P9-DNO-217

DEC 2017

CH

THE FOLD

A REDBONE NOVEL

T. STYLES

NATIONAL BEST SELLING AUTHOR OF *RAUNCHY*

By T. STYLES

CHECK OUT OTHER TITLES BY THE CARTEL PUBLICATIONS

4   *THE FOLD*

WWW.THECARTELPUBLICATIONS.COM

By T. STYLES   5

THE FOLD

BY

T. STYLES

PUBLISHER'S NOTE:
This book is a work of fiction. Names,
characters, businesses,
Organizations, places, events and incidents
are the product of the
Author's imagination or are used fictionally.
Any resemblance of
Actual persons, living or dead, events, or
locales are entirely coincidental.

Library of Congress Control Number: 2017947246

ISBN 10: 1945240016

ISBN 13: 978-1945240010

Cover Design: Davida Baldwin
www.oddballdsgn.com

www.thecartelpublications.com
First Edition
Printed in the United States of America

What's Up Fam,

Happy Summer!! I'm so happy that we are into the Summer of '17 with so many big things popping off! Our latest web series, "Bmore Chicks" just premiered! We're only two episodes in, so you have time to catch up! Trust me, you do not want to miss this show! It airs every Tuesday at 8PM on YouTube.

Now...The Fold! I had been glued to these bloody pages from the moment I got the privilege to read them. T. Styles outdid herself yet again with this thriller. I could not put it down until the end and you won't want to either!!

With that being said, keeping in line with tradition, we want to give respect to a vet or trailblazer paving the way. In this novel, we would like to recognize:

Charlamagne Tha God

Lenard McKelvey AKA Charlamagne Tha God is the TV personality and radio host on the nationally syndicated morning talk show, "The Breakfast Club". Just recently Charlamagne penned his first novel, "Black

Privilege: Opportunity Comes To Those Who Create It". It is a comedic and highly opinionated novel on the quickest way to be successful. It is a good read, so make sure you check it out!

Aight, get to it. I'll catch you in the next novel.

Be Easy!

Charisse "C. Wash" Washington
Vice President
The Cartel Publications
www.thecartelpublications.com
www.facebook.com/publishercwash
Instagram: publishercwash
www.twitter.com/cartelbooks
www.facebook.com/cartelpublications
Follow us on Instagram: Cartelpublications
#CartelPublications
#UrbanFiction
#PrayForCeCe
#CharlamagneThaGod

CARTEL URBAN CINEMA'S
3rd WEB SERIES

BMORE CHICKS
@ Pink Crystal Inn

NOW PLAYING:

Via

YOUTUBE

Don't Want To Wait? Purchase the ENTIRE
Season via DVD Today!

www.youtube.com/user/tstyles74
www.cartelurbancinema.com
www.thecartelpublications.com

THE FOLD

CARTEL URBAN CINEMA's ^{2nd} MOVIE

MOTHER MONSTER
The movie based off the book,
"RAUNCHY"
by
T. Styles
Now Available on You Tube
Available to Download via VIMEO
www.cartelurbancinema.com and
www.thecartelpublications.com

CARTEL URBAN CINEMA'S 1st WEB SERIES

THE WORST OF US
(Season One & Season Two)

NOW AVAILABLE:
YOUTUBE / STREAMING/ DVD

www.youtube.com/user/tstyles74
www.cartelurbancinema.com
www.thecartelpublications.com

By T. STYLES   13

CARTEL URBAN CINEMA'S 1st MOVIE

PITBULLS IN A SKIRT – THE MOVIE

www.cartelurbancinema.com and
www.amazon.com
www.thecartelpublications.com

THE FOLD

#TheFold

THE FOLD

PROLOGUE
CRESCENT FALLS
THE PAST

T *hey sat mostly in darkness.*
        And funk.

The odor, resembling death, hung in the air, penetrating everything breathable, including the dirty sheets.

Their unbounded wrists were still raw from leather handcuffs that recently tied them to beds. Although no longer hooked to the mattresses like criminals, they were far from free.

"Something's wrong," Courtney whispered as she paced the cool floor within a room that held twenty bunks. Her shoulder length hair so matted it resembled dreadlocks. "Why haven't they been feeding us? Have they forgotten about us? Have they — "

"Shut the fuck up!" A harsh voice called out across the room. "The last thing we want them to do is come back now." Giovanna rubbed her sunken eyes and looked crazily around. "Just...just shut up before you make shit worse! I can't deal with you right now." She placed her hands on her ears, Courtney's voice too irritating to be heard for a long time.

By T. STYLES   17

Courtney slapped a hand over her lips but it did her no good. She was horrified. "We gonna die," Courtney continued. "And I don't wanna...I don't wanna go like this." She paused only to rub her throat until it was almost raw. "And the thirst is...is killing me. I just want one sip of water."

Laverne, another patient said, "Maybe you should...um – "

"No!" Giovanna yelled as she gazed across the room at Laverne who had taken to drinking her own urine to fight thirst. "We aren't like you. We will never go that far."

Laverne laughed at the foolish women. Unlike the others she had done many things to live, including poking herself with needles and drinking her own blood for protein. So she could care less what they said, in her mind she was a survivor. "Of course you're not like me." She nodded. "Not yet anyway, but if we stay here much longer you will be."

Suddenly the doors flew open and other patients who wore blue hospital gowns just like the girls, with no shoes, were pushed inside.

"Men aren't supposed to be in here!" Giovanna yelled. Before she could dispute further, the orderlies who brought them inside slammed the doors shut before locking the latch. And once again, just like that, they were submerged in partial darkness.

"You aren't supposed to be here!" Giovanna repeated to the skinniest one, her long finger wagging his way. *"Especially with what's been going on. I don't feel safe."*

Morton gave a deep ugly laugh. *"That's why we're here. Because of what's going on. If anything I should be blaming you bitches for all of this."*

"Us?" Giovanna pointed at herself. *"You don't even know me."* She crossed her arms over her chest. *"Some of us were raped and — "*

"I hear all that but we didn't fuckin' rape you!" Lewis, one of the three yelled. *"They put us in here because we didn't like what we saw."* He pointed at the floor. Unlike the others, he was virtually skin and bones with braids so bushy you couldn't see the rows.

"And 'cause we wouldn't participate," Morton added. He was so tall the others had to look up at him. *"Now I wish I did get a little bit of pussy from one of these bitches in this place. Maybe I wouldn't be in whatever this shit is."*

"So...you knew?" Courtney asked, jaw trembling. *"About what they did to us?"*

"Ain't you listening? Everybody knows," Lewis responded, moving like a man suddenly on a mission. *"Which is why we getting outta here. Shit getting too thick."* He rushed away from them and between two twin beds where a window sat in the middle. Trying to escape he

pushed and pulled at the pane but it wouldn't give. "Fuck!"
He yelled. "They ain't trying to let us go!"

"That's 'cause we ain't meant to get let go," Laverne
said, her lips still wet with her own urine. "We meant to
starve and then die."

They all looked at one another, their expressions a soft
shade of currant due to the moonlight shining through the
purple tinted windowpanes.

"I can't believe this is happening." Courtney yelled,
placing her hands on the sides of her head. "I don't wanna
die! I don't wanna fucking die!" She was repeating her
madness and losing whatever sanity she possessed.

While simultaneously irritating the fuck out of
everybody.

Afraid she was about to make matters worse, Lewis
rushed up to her. "I'm not about to let you fuck up my
plans!" He yelled. "So I suggest you calm down before I
smash your jaw until it's sand. I've done it before."

He took a step closer and Giovanna blocked him with her
body. But Lewis remained standing, watching as if he was
prepared to kill Courtney and Giovanna second. With wild
darting eyes, for some reason Lewis took a deep breath and
walked away. Maybe he wouldn't kill her. For the moment
anyway.

"They were in their offices, thinking about the best way to deal with us," Morton interjected. "So fighting with each other ain't helping." He paused. "Has anybody stopped to wonder why we got separated from the rest of the patients?"

"'Cause we the best of the worst," Laverne added, walking toward the others. "If I had to pick a place to start it would be there."

Silence.

"And we remember more than most too. Still got most of our brain cells. Eight percent of everybody else in Crescent has had them fried." She continued, clearing her throat. "At least that's what I think."

Morton paced. "We have to —

Suddenly the door opened again and three more men were shoved inside. Like the others, all were wearing blue hospital gowns and hadn't eaten in days. With the new additions to the room, they now made twenty-three.

The doors closed again abruptly.

"FUCK YOU!" Porter yelled, banging on the closed door. "Fuck all of you!" When it was obvious the orderlies were gone, and that his rage was misplaced, he turned around and looked at everyone. "Fuck going on?" He waited for an answer. "Why they push us in here with females?"

"I'll tell you what's going on. They are trying to clean up what they did to us." She paused. "It was two of them at first," Courtney said out of nowhere, her eyes looking at nothing in particular. "They would come into the room and say they were taking me to treatment. But they never did." Tears rolled down her cheeks. One by one they fucked me in every available space on my body. Leaving me with their fluids that would crust in the morning because I was locked to the bed and wasn't able to wash myself." She sighed. "Guess they liked what they were doing 'cause they would come back night after night, like I was a carnival ride, sometimes bringing three or four more at a time."

Morton walked away, his fingers pushing through his thick black hair. "Look, I'm...I'm..." An apology couldn't fully leave his lips because as far as he was concerned it wasn't his fault. "I get what happened to you. But why all this? I feel like they know something we don't."

"And where that new doctor?" Lewis asked. "The one who been asking questions about how they been treating us?"

"Even if he still here I heard they 'bout to fire him." Laverne shrugged. "Apparently he give a fuck too much and they prefer people like that gone in Crescent."

"Wow." Giovanna shook her head. "All this during Christmas."

"These people don't care about the holidays," Laverne said. "They want blood and for us to remain silent. Forever.

I heard from Vivica that the doc was threatening to go to the police. And the press about the rapes." She paused. "I don't even know why that doctor works here. I hear he's rich."

"So what's — "

Again…the door opened.

And this time its visitors brought with them the threat of death.

CHAPTER ONE

THE PRESENT

FARAH

"I can tell you've thought about me. A lot. It's all in your eyes."

Cutie Tudy, aka Tudy Ranger, had sent her foster mother on a hunt for a woman Melinda was sure didn't exist.

The infamous Farah Cotton.

So to appease the young girl, Melinda was set on proving the girl wrong.

Cutie sat in the back of Jones's car, a friend of her foster mother Melinda, who drove so slowly a woman pushing a baby carriage would've gotten to their destination faster. As they continued up the main road and along a private tree lined street, Jones looked back at Cutie and then Melinda. He didn't feel like going anywhere, definitely not to a place unknown.

When the car parked the property seemed larger than they expected and somewhat horrific. Without even knocking on the door, Melinda already in fear of her and Cutie's lives. Why had she allowed a child to talk her into hunting for a ghost? A figment of her imagination?

Afraid for her foster child's well being, Melinda looked at her in the backseat and said, "Cutie, I don't know about this." She gazed at an address in a phonebook, which she'd taken from her foster daughter earlier. The numbers on the gate matched which appeared to give a signal that they were in the right place. "This doesn't seem real."

"I don't care if it is or not," Jones interjected. "At this point I've been driving you both around for hours. A shot of pussy not gonna be nearly enough for this fare." He pointed downward.

"You talk that shit when we get back to the house," Melinda said grabbing at his crotch, stroking it gently, and calming him down instantly. "I bet you'll be singing a whole new tune then."

Cutie was annoyed with them both. "Can you go to the intercom thing at the gate, ma?" Cutie asked with wide eyes. "Please?"

Melinda tilted her head. "Oh now I'm ma?" In the past Cutie made it known that she was not her real mother, despite the child being in her care. Suddenly, when she wanted something she was all the rage again. It was very suspicious.

"I'm begging you." Cutie positioned her hands as if she were praying. "I gotta know. I just gotta."

It was at that moment that Melinda truly realized she cared for the weird child. Why else would she allow her to run her all over town? Melinda shook her head, eased out of the car and approached the intercom with Cutie hot on her heels. Afraid, although she wasn't sure why, Melinda pressed the button on the device in an attempt to connect with someone inside.

"Hello," the female voice said from the speaker. "How can I help you?"

Cutie looked at Melinda to respond but when she didn't answer quickly enough she stepped up. "Uh…is Farah Cotton there?"

Silence.

Melinda looked down at Cutie with a knowing look. Something told her they would meet anybody except the great Farah Cotton. So why couldn't she walk away and yank the child who was left in her care? Melinda was almost certain that just like the other house they visited in an attempt to find Farah earlier that day, only to be turned away, that this one would be the same. Still she wanted to put the vampire idea out of Cutie's mind. That alone gave her enough courage to take the first step.

"You have the wrong address," the voice said. "Get off the property."

Melinda grabbed Cutie's hand harshly and yanked her in the direction of the car. "Now will you please leave this alone?"

Cutie shook her off and returned to the intercom. Pressing the button again she said, "Is Bones there?"

"Who is this?" The voice asked more angrily. "And what are you still doing on the property?"

"My name is Cutie...and I'm a friend of Mooney."

A few seconds later the voice returned. "How do you know Mooney?"

Melinda and Cutie's eyes widened believing they were getting somewhere after all. "She was a friend of mine," Cutie said. "But she died a little while ago."

A few seconds passed and the gates rolled open allowing them entry. Accepting the invitation, Cutie dipped inside, fearing they would shut them again without her closer to meeting her idol. Of course Melinda trailed behind the teen, arms flailing as she tried to grab her and pull her back into the safety of the car.

"Hold up, Cutie!" She called out. "I don't trust this place!"

She could run her mouth all she wanted the girl was on a mission, to finally meet the woman of her dreams. And after running for what seemed like forever, Cutie happened upon a double black lacquer door. It was so large it was intimidating and before long a handsome man with neat dreads running down his back exited with three women at his side. "What you say about Mooney?" He asked, his voice booming with authority. He stood over the child in an intimidating manner.

"Are you…are you Bones?" Cutie questioned, eyes glistening.

He looked back at the women before focusing on Melinda and Cutie again. Who was this bitch who thought she knew him? "I asked what you say about Mooney?"

"Uh, she was murdered a few weeks ago. Her funeral was today and she's a friend of mine." Cutie paused, sadness visiting her again due to the loss of the old woman. "Well, she *was* a friend of mine." Blinking back tears she continued. "Did you know her?"

"You mean outside of her trying to break into my house, forcing me to chop off her arm?"

Cutie stumbled. "You were the one who cut her?"

"Listen, I don't know what Mooney told you but you better forget everything she said. The woman was off her rocker anyway." He pointed at her sternly. "Don't be spreading lies."

"No problem, we're out of here," Melinda said trying to snatch Cutie away from the volatile scene. "Come on, we have to go home."

"Get off of me!" Cutie yelled pulling away. She moved closer to the man and it was obvious that the child was fearless, a trait that was bound to get her in trouble. "She wrote about you in her journal, Bones. I know almost everything there is to know about you."

Bones glared at her and stepped closer. Now the kid had gone way too far. "Mooney wrote about me? In that book right there?" He pointed.

"Yes." She swallowed the lump in her throat.

He snatched it away and flipped through the pages. He could tell that it had been read many times, the pages barely holding onto the spine. It was also obvious to all that the property now belonged to him.

"But there's more," Melinda said, sensing they were in danger now that he believed that he held onto the only book of his story in his hands. "A whole series of them are back at my house." She wanted him to know if he killed them the secret was still out.

Bones smiled sinisterly. "How convenient."

Suddenly the door opened wider and a light skin woman with a red chiffon flowing dress exited the premises. She looked regal and was truly the most beautiful woman Cutie had ever seen. "Did she write about me too, little girl?" The woman questioned.

"Are you Farah Cotton?" Cutie asked, as she felt herself on the verge of crying. Her knees buckled a little and she could barely stand straight. This was not happening. She could not be real.

Farah nodded. "Yes...I am."

Cutie ran up to her and hugged her hard before separating. "Mooney spoke so much about you." She said excitedly. "You are the most interesting woman I know!"

Farah frowned because she didn't know her to make that statement. "You shouldn't have come here," Farah said seriously, pity all in her eyes for the child. "You should never have come."

Cutie's heart rocked in her chest upon hearing the response. It definitely wasn't what she had in mind. "Are your friends...The Fold? Are you vampires?"

Farah looked back at Bones and down at Cutie. Now she'd said too much to ever leave. Although she didn't answer when Cutie glanced at their clothing and saw tiny T's and F's embedded in the fabric she had her answer.

And it was all the confirmation Cutie needed.

Farah gripped Cutie's hand and pushed open the huge black lacquer doors as they entered the mansion briskly. They were stopped short when seven members of The Fold approached them, looking at Cutie sinisterly and as if she were a new toy.

First there was Nicola, who smiled at the girl, ready to drink her blood or eat her pussy, her choice. Then there was Denny, Nicola's right hand who was only happy if she was having sex, with someone, anyone to hear her tell it.

Then there was Eve, a cutie with a passion for gasoline and matches. It wasn't enough for her to enjoy a fireplace or too. She wasn't fully satisfied unless she was starting fires that destroyed buildings, cities or living things. Nothing got her wetter than arson.

Next to them was Wesley, who Farah used to enjoy sexually from time to time until Bones forbid any of them to play with her, something that had always been a past time for other members.

To Wesley's left was Vivica, a beautiful but amazing liar. She would fib about everything from the color of the sky to someone else's life. It didn't matter to her. Just as long as she was lying and people were listening.

But it was Gregory with his serial rapist ways and Swanson with his serial killer ways that were really interested in the young girl. As long as Dr. Weil, The Fold's protector, kept everyone's condition at bay via medication and pain therapy, everyone was safe. But if anything changed it would be hell on earth.

"Aye, Cotton," who's the new girl," Gregory asked stroking his large penis which stiffened in his jeans. "She playing and staying right? Cause I need a new flavor 'round here."

"Yeah," Swanson grinned. "She look like her blood might be kinda sweet." He sucked his teeth. "What's up, sexy?" He asked Cutie. "You wanna —"

"She's off limits!" Farah yelled, dragging her past them.

They frowned.

"Since when this happen?" Gregory yelled as she continued down the hall. "She here, which means she's fuck-a-ble!"

When Cutie turned around the door opened again and she saw Melinda being whisked into the mansion, in the opposite direction of her and Farah. "Cutie!" Melinda called out. "What's happening?"

"I don't know, ma!" She said. "I'm sorry. I'm so sorry!"

"She good!" Bones said pulling her away. "You coming with me though."

Hearing her foster mother's frantic voice, she realized in her youthful foolishness that she made a grave mistake that could cost them their lives, and yet for the moment she was too in awe, too fascinated with it all, to understand. Besides, Farah was squeezing her fingers so tightly they throbbed. How could she get away from her?

And would she drink her blood too?

The scent of the mansion was thick.

A mixture of leather, vanilla and apples tickled the senses and Cutie wondered if it had been deliberate. To make her feel at home, which surprisingly with Farah holding her hand she already had.

When Farah walked them toward huge double doors inside the house, Cutie couldn't believe her eyes as she took in the intricate patterns carved inside the blood red wooden doors. Only five minutes in the mansion and already it was larger than her imagination.

Mystical.

Fascinating.

Alluring.

At their destination, Farah unlocked the door and yanked her inside, closing it behind them. Cutie's breath stagnated in her throat as she looked at Farah's exquisite Victorian style bedroom.

Dark yellow walls, black and gold wall lamps with red night shades all seemed to put on a show for the magnificent black carved bed that dominated thirty percent of the space.

It was like nothing Cutie had ever seen.

Taking a deep breath, Farah sat on the edge of her bed and said, "Come... sit next to me. We must talk."

Cutie remained in place. As if moving would wake her up from the dream she believed she was having.

Farah took a deep breath. "Are you scared of me?"

She shook her head no.

"Then come. I hate asking twice."

THE FOLD

Cutie trudged slowly toward her, feet flopping under her body like clown shoes. She felt so silly she released a sigh of relief when the bed, which she had to climb on, held her weight. At least she wouldn't look stupid when she moved.

Farah smiled. "I can tell you've thought about me. A lot. It's all in your eyes."

Cutie nodded again.

"But there's a saying some live by. And that is, be careful what you wish for, you just might get it."

Cutie looked around, her eyes refusing to rest on one thing in particular because everything was too beautiful. There were so many things she wanted to say to her when she finally met her and now...well...she realized she was out of her league. How foolish she felt.

"Is Mooney really dead?" Farah asked.

Cutie nodded. "Yes, saw it myself."

"How?"

"This boy I know shot her."

"Let me guess. For getting into other people's business?"

Cutie nodded yes.

Farah looked away. "Silly old woman. I warned her."

Slowly Farah stood up and moved toward her terrace, looking out into the land behind the mansion. She always hoped Mooney got on with her life and now she knew she didn't. As Cutie observed her she couldn't help but feel like she was in the presence of a star.

All of the stories.

All of the tales and now she was realizing Farah Cotton was real.

"Is it true?" Cutie asked. "That you drink blood?"

Farah turned toward her. "What did you think would happen when you came here?"

"I don't know." She shrugged. "I just...wanted to meet you I guess. Didn't really think it through that much."

The bedroom door flew open.

Bones entered first, his black slacks and shirt with TF laid smoothly against his fit body, his neat dreads resting over his shoulders. Cutie could see why any girl would fall for him, but it was the tall snack behind him that made Cutie's knees weak. He was Phoenix, a 24-year-old freak and she had to have him.

Quickly she adjusted her hair by fingering the curls to be sure she looked presentable or good enough to finger fuck at the very least. Melinda always said Cutie was too fast for her age but she didn't care. In her opinion she was winning. With her hormones in rage she wanted what she wanted and now she wanted him.

"I thought Phoenix could show your new friend around the mansion." Bones said to Farah. "Since she'll be staying for *awhile*." He gave Farah a knowing look that Cutie, with her foolish mind tried to decipher.

Basically the child was a hostage and she was clueless.

"Yeah...let me show you a good time." Phoenix winked at Cutie who giggled. "I'ma make you love me."

Farah swallowed the lump in her throat. Nothing about her getting up with him made sense because Phoenix was a monster and Farah knew it. "I'm not sure, Bones. She—"

"She'll be fine," Bones said harshly.

Farah nodded. "Yes...of course...I'm sure she'd enjoy herself."

Phoenix extended his hand and Cutie grabbed it so quickly she almost yanked it off. When they disappeared Bones closed the door and approached Farah. "I'm starting to not trust your judgment anymore." He pointed a finger at her and she slapped it away. Smiling, he smacked her to her knees for being too grown. "Ms. Cotton. Did you forget who I am?"

She looked up at him, eyes glaring.

"Never disrespect me again." He extended his hand and she accepted…slowly rising to her feet.

"What do you want, Bones? Did you hurt the girl's mother? And the driver?"

"You already know they're dead. And I should've killed that old bitch Mooney when I had a chance too." He raised the book. "And now look. All of our secrets are out there for the world to see." He moved closer. "Mooney actually wrote about what goes on in this house. In our lives! I can't believe this shit!" He said through clenched teeth. "And now we exposed."

Farah sighed. "You haven't even read the journal yet."

"But I will." He pointed at her with the spine of the book. "And I better not find anything you told her about me in this bitch either."

"I didn't, Bones."

He nodded and placed his cool hand on the side of her face, stared into her eyes and stormed out.

DR. WEIL

He had three women under his desk. Denny, Nicola and Eve. One licked the left ball, the other the right, and the third the tip of his dick. One of the perks of running The Fold was the unlimited amount of sexual pleasures and he took advantage of them all. But for him ecstasy came not in reaching an orgasm but from the power being the boss warranted. He used to care about medicine, and now he was consumed with sexuality.

Looking up at him like three little birds, he willed himself to cum inside Nicola's mouth. When he came on her tongue she turned her head and kissed Denny and then Eve as they all tasted a little of the king's icing. Long strings of nut connecting them. It was perfect timing too because there was a knock on the door.

"Thanks, ladies," he said. "You all can leave now."

On the way out Bones walked inside, glared at Nicola, Denny and Eve and slammed the door behind himself. "Still having all the fun huh?"

Dr. Weil smirked. "And you don't?"

"Ain't you heard? I'm a one woman man."

Dr. Weil shook his head and chuckled. "Then you a fool. So what you want, Bones?"

"We have guests."

Dr. Weil shrugged. "I heard. And you know my rules on bringing people here." He stood up and fastened his pants. "Once they in, its for life. So where are the bodies?"

"I took care of two of them but the child is still alive."

Dr. Weil glared. "What does that mean?"

"Mooney wrote about us in a book." He paused. "And I think it's documented about what goes on here. The hunt, the business...everything. My only problem is I don't know who else knows. I just want to make sure that the child gives me all the books."

Dr. Weil glared and rushed over to him. "You assured me Mooney was dead."

"And I—"

Dr. Weil stole him in the jaw, shook his hand and wiped it with the black towel on his desk.

Bones glared.

"You're sloppy, Bones. Didn't used to be, but I guess that's changed now."

Bones wiped the blood off his mouth and leaned against the wall. "That's not true."

"It is!" He yelled. "You aren't the man you used to be." He pointed at him. "The one that I could depend on. Guess Farah has you weak at the knees. But it's not like I don't understand."

Bones' jaw twitched. "Invited Farah to one of your little dinners again?" He paused. "Cause we all know that's what you want. Me out the picture so you can have my woman. Which—"

"Nigga, if I wanted you gone you wouldn't exist." He tossed the towel in Bones' face. "Farah wants a real man. You and I both know it." He smirked. "Besides, if something happened to me who would run The Fold? You? Carlton who too busy sniffing behind Mayoni to know what needs to be done?" He paused. "If I left it would be like releasing a hundred crazies onto the streets." He paused. "I keep people sane and cared for not you." He laughed. "As a matter of fact, I don't know what I have you around for anymore. Now get out my space. You smell of defeat."

Bones dropped the towel and stormed out.

CHAPTER TWO

MISSISSIPPI

SLADE

"Let's just enjoy the moment."

Rain pounded on the windows as Slade stood at the foot of the bed, his hands grasping his eight-month-old pregnant girlfriend's waist as he pumped into her from behind. His chocolate muscular frame was fully engaged as he looked down at her braids, hanging along the sides of her angelic face as she moaned.

Unlike some men who chose to ignore their pregnant women sexually during this period, he was a country nigga, who realized the pussy was best during this time.

Hot...warm...and tight.

As he stared down at her chocolate body moving to the beat of his pumps, his flesh trembled at how she responded to him. Pleasure given. Pleasure received, was his motto. Add to that, he was on the verge of busting.

Yep, sex with ole girl was always official.

But as vicious as her pussy was, Memory Spencer could never be...would never be...Farah Cotton. And for that she would always fall short in his eyes.

Turning her head to the left, she clutched the high thread count sheets and said, "Damn, Slade...I love you." She backed into him harder. "So fucking much...never leave me." Sweat dripped everywhere.

He smiled and impelled her a little harder to silence her. He would never be in love with her so it was his duty to get that idea out of her mind. It didn't matter that she was carrying a child he truly wanted. He wasn't feeling her in that way, which to some may be fucked up.

"I wanna hear you say the words," she wept. "Even if you don't mean them." She paused. "Please, Slade. Just once."

"Stop with all that," he said. "Let's just enjoy the moment."

"You'll never leave me right, Slade?"

He rolled his eyes and instead of answering, squeezed her ass cheeks and raised them a little so he could see the pinkness of her pussy from behind as he drilled into her wetness.

It was a miracle!

Suddenly she wasn't getting on his nerves by asking a thousand questions, which at the end of the day was his plan. Fuck her quiet. Talking about the future with a woman who didn't make his heart pump with love was annoying and something in his spirit told him she knew it too.

Besides, Memory didn't have a mind of her own. She was *Miss Whatever You Like.*

If Slade wanted to watch the game she was, *whatever you like.*

If Slade wanted to stay over his brother's house for the weekend she was, *whatever you like.*

When Slade wanted to fuck her in the ass and watch her suck his dick seconds later, again she was *whatever you like.*

There was no fight in her and he needed a woman who said what was on her mind despite the prospect of losing him if she said the wrong thing. Although she was beautiful and there was no denying it, she didn't make him desire. She didn't have her own mind and that was severely unattractive. As hard as he tried, he was losing respect for her and in a place deep inside his heart; he started to hate her slightly for her shortcomings.

"FUCCCKKKKKK!" He moaned as he released his juice inside her hot body, another pro for having a pregnant girlfriend. The last thing you could do was get a bitch pregnant twice.

Fully satisfied, he slapped her right ass cheek. "Damn that shit was right." He pulled out of her, grabbed the white hand towel off the bed and wiped his wet, thick dick before tossing it on the floor.

He wanted to relax until she came again at him with the one hundred questions. "Where do you go when you leave me? Mentally?" She crawled in bed next to him. "You're so...I guess, different lately."

He grinned. "What you talking 'bout now, girl? You want me to break you off again?" He asked jokingly.

She crawled on top of him and placed her hand on his face. "I don't have all of you, Slade. And I'm realizing that's, something I need. Especially while being pregnant."

He rolled his eyes.

The chick was blowing him.

"I know you don't like to get heavy but ..." She took a deep breath. "I guess I want to do whatever I can and be the best for—"

"Yourself." He interrupted. "Be the best for yourself, Memory. Never for me because you could never know all the things I want."

She frowned, having gotten nowhere quick. "So when you gonna make me your wife then? Tell me that!"

Now it was time to bounce.

He eased out of bed, slipped into his grey sweats and white beater. She frowned at his gear. "So you wearing a slut outfit out the house, Slade? After we just had sex? I mean, where you going dressed like that?"

He shook his head and grabbed his car keys and wallet off the dresser. "You want some Butter Pecan ice cream with honey? I'ma stop by the store right quick."

She sighed and crossed her arms over her chest while pouting. What she wanted was some answers to her questions coupled with a ring.

He shrugged. "Well I'ma go grab some anyway. I'll be right back."

Slade sat in his burgundy Escalade in front of 7-Eleven just staring at people coming and going. Fucking Memory was always a delight but the last thing he wanted was to go home, even if he was always in the mood for part two. Instead, he glanced over at a pint of Butter Pecan ice cream that sat in the passenger seat that although rock hard at first, was beginning its softening process.

"Where are you Farah?" He said to himself. "Where—"

KNOCK. KNOCK. KNOCK.

Startled, Slade reached for the hammer under his seat, preparing to blast whoever was rapping at his window when he saw his youngest brother wearing blue coveralls soiled with motor oil. Relieved, Slade released the handle of the weapon and rolled the window down on his side. "What you doing, nigga?" Slade asked. "I almost shot your brows off."

Audio laughed and tapped the car. "You ain't shooting nobody, shut your bitch ass up. When the last time you shot anything anyway?"

Slade sat back in his fawn colored leather seat, and wiped his hand down his baldhead in relief. "Where you going?"

"Killa got some burgers on the grill and Major stopping by later with the beer." Audio hit the hood of the truck, walked toward the passenger door and hopped in. "You going right? Take me over there."

Slade looked around. "Where your car?"

"This chick I be fucking with dropped me off. She just—"

"Please say you not hitting off your boss's wife again?"

"Nah...I been stopped fucking her." He winked. "She just ain't stop fucking me yet." Audio laughed, opened the Butter Pecan ice cream and slopped it up with the lid. "Damn, this shit good as fuck!"

Future's voice blasted through the speakers in Killa's backyard as he flipped over burgers, hot dogs and chicken wings. A few of their cousins were in attendance but it was the three brothers who were keeping court with one another, as if nothing else was going on in the world.

The pit's smoke covered his brothers when Killa looked over at them while he played chef. But it was Slade's uneasy expression, even through the thick grey charcoal clouds, that caught his attention. He seemed to be somewhere else mentally and Killa wanted to know where. With his meat looking right, he snatched his beer off the grill and plopped between them. "So you 'bout to do it ain't you?" He took a sip. "And ain't no need in lying 'cause I know my brothers. Just be real with me."

Slade looked at him for a second, shook his head and gazed downward. "I don't know yet."

Immediately Audio, who finally got what was being said, grew excited. Turning toward them both he said, "Let's do it! Please, man. It ain't like we got shit going on down here!"

Slade frowned. "You don't even know what we talking about."

"Yeah I do." He grinned. "Farah Cotton."

Slade was impressed. "Even if you know that don't mean you going."

Audio sat his beer down. "Come on, man! Look at my fucking life." He stared at them both, pleading with his eyes for mercy. "I change oil in nigga's cars for a living! This ain't even me." He focused on Slade. "You gotta save me and you do that with an adventure. Plus I'm the only one who knows where she lives. Remember, I been to that house." He pointed at him. "You haven't."

Slade laughed heavily for the first time in a long time. Slowly the laugh simmered before fading away. He realized that he wasn't happy with his life. In fact, he was fucking miserable. He always knew it but there was no turning back. "I don't want anything happening to you." He looked at Audio. "I don't want anything happening to either of you." He looked at Killa.

"We feel the same way," Killa said. "But if you go alone that's a bad look. At the end of the day we can't lose no more people in this family, Slade," Killa paused. "So we gotta take the ride. It's as simple as that."

Slade thought about the violence that awaited them, courtesy of The Fold, if they went. They agreed to stay away and this was breaking the rules. Their mother already died from cancer, the last thing he needed was to lose another brother. "Nah, man—"

"Listen, Slade, I got a kid in D.C. who I haven't been able to see because of that pact you made with The Fold to stay out the city," Killa interrupted. "Now

I agreed not to go back because I didn't want anything happening to family. But I want to see my kid and not just through pictures. Plus if you getting into danger you need your brothers at your side. I don't even know why I gotta say all this 'cause we going."

"All I'ma add is this," Audio added. "If you two niggas leave me I'ma purposely get into trouble in the 'Ssissippi just because. I'm talkin' bout all kinds of shit too. Robberies…fights…maybe fuck a few extra bitches when they ain't watching just for fun. Don't even get me started with the — "

"Aight, man!" Slade said as all three laughed. He looked into their eyes. "So it's settled. We goin' back to D.C." He sighed. "But don't expect a happy reception when we get there. Them niggas from The Fold gonna do everything in their power to kill us." He took a deep, long breath. "Okay…now I gotta tell Memory."

"Telling her is the least of your troubles," Audio said.

"He right 'bout that," Killa added. "First you gotta tell Major."

CHAPTER THREE

FARAH

"What I do to my man in our bedroom is our business."

Bones struck her again and she couldn't get it out of her mind.

Lately he had been harsher than ever, as if he wanted to beat the pride out of her and it was working. Adding to her burdens was Cutie being in the house who Farah had taken an interest in because of Mooney. Her days had always been dark but now they seemed bleak and without hope. In her opinion there was only one person who could bring her light.

Slade Baker.

It had been over two years since she'd seen or heard from him and to be honest she was angry. Why hadn't he fought for her? Why hadn't he done more to stay near? Although she knew he would be murdered the moment his southern boots stepped foot in the city, she wanted to hold him just once.

But she made an agreement with the devil.

And the devil's name was Mayoni.

If Mayoni was nothing else it could definitely be said that she was a rider when it came to making sure Bones was happy. And so after so many years she still forced Farah into a wall that would forever break her heart. Denounce her relationship with Slade to make Bones happy, or she'd send a pack of Fold members to his house to kill him before murdering her siblings, Shadow and Mia, her only living relatives.

"Slade, are you even thinking about me?" Farah asked to herself in the shower.

"Slade?" Mayoni repeated, having entered the bathroom without an invite. "What about that nigga?"

Farah, who was stunned she was almost caught, remained silent for a moment. "Mayoni, is that you?"

"Who else?" When Farah peaked out of the red stained glass she saw Mayoni holding her black towel. "Farah, what about Slade?"

Farah snatched it from her, covered her body and walked toward the mirror. "What do you want, bitch?"

Mayoni stood behind her as Farah swiped a hand on the mirror to wipe away the steam. "Just so you know, I'm suggesting to Bones that we restart Shikar. We haven't gotten fresh blood in over six months and the others are getting restless with sucking on each other. It's time for a hunt. And in case you haven't realized it, they have eyes on that little girl. They'll be slurping her blood out and fucking her too if you don't be careful."

"She's underage."

"And?"

Farah shook her head. "Do what you want, Mayoni. But Dr. Weil said he wasn't feeling Shikar."

"You must not know the man who shares your bed." She looked her up and down. "Well...shares your bed sometimes." She paused. "Anyway, Bones can be very convincing when he wants to."

"I think you're out of touch with what's going on. Dr. Weil and Bones are not as close as they used to be."

Mayoni rolled her eyes. "I wonder why?" She looked at her as if she were a slut with a stank pussy. "If you ask me this is all your fault. After all, you love seducing men don't you?" She placed her hands on her hips. "Even Dr. Weil."

Farah looked at her and crossed her arms over her chest. "Get the fuck out my bathroom."

"Are you holding your end of the bargain, Farah? Are you satisfying Bones and ensuring that he's happy? Because as you remember that's the only reason why Slade and —"

Farah glared. "What I do to my man in our bedroom is our business."

"Now you and me both know that's a lie." She giggled. "Because I'm the silent partner in you and Bones' relationship. Never forget it."

Farah laughed hysterically. "I finally understand exactly what's going on." Farah pointed at her. "Did you use to fuck Bones or something?" Mayoni moved to slap her and Farah gripped her wrist before pushing her backwards.

Having caught the tail end of a heated argument that could've gotten violent, Bones walked in and eyed them both harshly. "When are you both going to tell me why you don't get along anymore? What aren't you saying? You used to be friends and now—"

"I have to go," Mayoni said leaving the bathroom abruptly.

When she was gone Farah looked at Bones. "And she was never my friend." She squinted a little when she saw a bruise on his face, courtesy of Dr. Weil. "Wait…what happened to your mouth?"

He glared. "Fuck that." He removed the towel from around her body and took a few seconds to enjoy the view. "Are you fucking Dr. Weil on the low? And be honest."

"What? No! Of course not. I'm not feeling him in anyway."

"Does he know that?"

Farah nodded her head. "Look, no man in here is allowed to touch me remember? Your rules. Your house. So I'm being honest."

He frowned. "You acting like you have a problem with it or something."

"I don't wanna talk about this. I'm very tired."

She tried to walk away and he snatched her back. "Turn around."

Knowing what he wanted, some pussy, she placed her hands on the sink. "Okay, Bones. Get it over with."

"Nah...I want you to cry for this dick."

"What? I, I don't understand."

"You understand perfectly so stop fucking around. Don't let your pride anger me." He released his penis and stroked it into stiffness. "You claim to be so in love with me that you'd do anything. Prove it. Cry."

"But—"

He smacked her and grabbed her warm, throbbing cheek when he was done. Her patience was running thin. It was like he was taking all of his darkness out on Farah, in an effort to dim her light. "Cry for this dick," he said through clenched teeth.

THE FOLD

"And if I don't?"

He pointed at her. "Oh, I forgot to tell you, Mia looks good. Lost a lot of weight too. Saw her the other day on my way to the city. Would be a shame for something to happen to her wouldn't it?"

And just like that, she was moved to tears. The truth was she knew he was about to threaten her family before he said a word. He did on a regular basis. But she needed a reason to cry and he gave her one.

"That's right, Farah," he moved her body so that her palms were now flat on the marble sink, her eyes viewing their reflection in the mirror. Just having him inside of her made her weep harder because she wanted him out of her body, so that she could have it to herself again. "There will come a time when you will finally realize the man you're with is all you need. Dr. Weil will never be able to fuck you like this with his old ass. I'm the only person who matters in your life."

Without another word he pounded her roughly. Nothing about their sex life was arousing to Farah because she had grown to hate him and everything he represented. But expressing her feelings meant death for everyone she loved.

"You gonna have my baby right?" He asked as he gripped her cheeks roughly again, causing red bruises to whelp up on her vanilla colored skin.

"Yes, Bones," she wept. "Anything you want."

"Yeah, you gonna have my seed." He bit into his bottom lip and continued to thrust briskly. "And she gonna be pretty as you and as dangerous as me." He slapped her ass cheek. "Fuckkkkk," he bit his lip hard. "Damn, your pussy get better by the pump. How you do that?"

She was emotionless.

He could care less if she talked at this point because a few minutes later he came inside her body, his clumpy nut rolling inside of her trying to find a way to her womb. Satisfied, he slapped her ass again and kissed the side of her cheek. "It was good. But I ain't gonna keep looking into your eyes and feeling unwanted, Farah. Especially when I'm surrounded by a house full of bitches just waiting to be by my side."

"Are you threatening to take the position back? The position I never asked for?" She paused. "'Cause if you are I can step down with pleasure. You'll have no trouble from me."

He gritted his teeth. "Being with me is an honor. You gonna find out the hard way." He stormed out.

When he left Farah locked the door, rushed to the toilet bowel and removed the lid. Next she grabbed a birth control case from inside, popped a pill and cupped some water from the sink to take the medicine. There was no way in the world she was having a baby, and definitely not one belonging to Bones.

With the pill in her system, killing any hopes of Bones' offspring, she sat on the toilet and cried. Remembering the last day she saw Slade, and the vow they both made to stay apart.

TWO YEARS EARLIER

A cool stream of water poured down Farah's face and awakened her roughly. She moaned a little until Bones grabbed a clump of her hair and positioned her gaze so that she could see directly out of the window. Bones had found Slade and wanted to hurt Farah by making her kill him. All because she didn't love him.

"Wake up, beautiful," Bones whispered in her ear. "Because I want you to see this shit."

When Farah opened her eyes she saw Carlton and Mayoni across the way at a park. Mayoni held a gun aimed at Slade, looked at the van and fired twice at his abdomen causing Slade to drop to the ground.

She fainted.

LATER THAT DAY

Farah lie face down on the bed in a mansion sobbing uncontrollably. Thoughts of when she first met Slade rushed to her mind and she missed him already. He was the love of her life and she would never get to see what they could've been together. To make matters worse Bones had dug his claws in her so deeply that to refuse him meant her brother and sister would also die.

What could she do but live in misery?

When she heard the door unlock she sat up in bed, afraid Bones was entering to rape her again. Instead it was Mayoni. "How you holding up?"

She frowned and rolled her eyes. "You killed the one man in the world I would've given my life for and you ask me that shit?" Her anger was bubbling at the surface and

THE FOLD

she thought about murder. *"You tell me, how would you feel if I took Carlton's life? Because I'm plotting as we speak."*

"Farah, you need to —"

"I need to what?" She yelled. *"I spent months in this bitch being somebody I'm not. I pretended to be meek so that Bones would feel stronger. And look where it got me! I will never, ever, love Bones after what he did! EVER. And if he plans on keeping me in this mansion I will tell him daily how much I hate him just to break his fucking heart."*

"You would do that even though it will kill him? Because there's nobody he wants more than you."

"Especially because he wants me."

Mayoni sighed. "Come with me, Farah. I have to show you something."

"Do I have a choice?" She sighed.

"No, but trust me."

LATER THAT DAY

Mayoni and Farah walked toward room 568 of a run down motel on the outskirts of Baltimore City. Before going inside Mayoni looked around to make sure no one was watching their moves. When the door opened Farah almost

By T. STYLES   61

fainted when she saw Carlton inside, holding a gun aimed at Slade.

Slade was alive!

The love of her life was breathing.

Overcome with joy she rushed up to him and wrapped her arms around his neck before kissing him passionately. "But I saw you." She kissed him again. "You were shot." She looked at Mayoni. "What's going on? I'm confused."

Was she dreaming?

Only to be reawakened in a nightmare?

"He'll explain everything," Mayoni said nodding at Slade. "You have thirty minutes to enjoy each other and not a second more."

She waited and Slade told her what happened.

He exhaled. "The Asian chick said when she fired I had to drop. At first I was going to try and overpower her and take the gun but she and that dude with the chewed up nose begged me to go along with the plan. I figured she had the weapon so if she wanted me dead I'd be gone already. So I played the part." He paused. "The next thing I know the van pulled off and they brought me here."

Farah was still confused but she didn't care. At least he was alive.

Afterwards they made love and he even allowed Farah to drink of his blood. At that moment he finally accepted who she was.

A vampire.

And they continued to explore each other until Mayoni knocked on the door and separated them.

Ending their time together.

CHAPTER FOUR

SLADE

"Because we blood. And I wanted to eye you face
to face like a man."

Red lights. Green lights. Yellow Lights.

They all highlighted the skin of the beautiful women in all shapes and tones dancing around Slade, Killa and Audio as they sat in the VIP section of the bar that Major owned. Simply called THE BAKERS, it brought the finest of dope boys and athletes from everywhere around these United States.

And after the night Slade had with Memory fussing about him not coming straight back with the ice cream she acted like she didn't want, something she never did, he could use the break. The way she carried on he was starting to believe she laid a trap with that sweet girl routine she gave him when they first started fucking. Now that she was pregnant, and wanted to control him, he figured she was free to let her chicken head shine.

Flashing boobs and pussy aside from the strippers, there was another reason Slade had for visiting Major and after two rounds of beer accompanied by tequila shots, it was time to get to the point of the night. "Major, we leaving for D.C. I gotta go get my bitch."

Major sat his beer on the table, looked at Audio, Killa and then Slade as if they were crazy. Perhaps they were. He thought his mind was playing tricks on him. Besides, he was just about to choose one of the flavors around him to fuck when he heard something about D.C. It just wasn't adding up. "Say that again."

"You heard me, man."

Major took a deep breath and rested his arms on his thighs, his hands clutched tightly in front of him. "So after everything we went through, with losing ma and —"

"That's not fair, man," Killa said pointing at him. "We didn't lose ma due to the beef with The Fold. You know that."

"Are you fucking serious?" He frowned at Killa. "It broke her heart when Knox died and all this shit happened in D.C.!" Major yelled causing the strippers to scurry. "And we broke her heart again when she lost her nephews! Now say that didn't have anything to do with The Fold and watch me crash your jaw." He pointed at him.

Slade wiped his hand down his face and sighed. He was trying to be understanding and yet the guilt bullet Major just dealt had him feeling like a creep.

Still, the facts were a little off.

True. He missed his mother and never got over losing her. True. Her face, loving hugs and the hope she had for their futures stuck with him always. But he would not be the man he knew he could be if he didn't go after the love of his life. And as crazy as she was, Farah Cotton was it for Slade.

"Before that cancer took ma's life, you heard what she said to me, Major." Slade looked into his eyes, trying to appeal to his heart. "To live my life, man. And I'm not doing that without Farah. Can't you see that?"

"Bullshit! You a traitor, nigga!"

There was no getting through to him.

Slade swatted at the air. "Well I'm going anyway and I'm just letting you know." He sat back. "I can't think of Farah being there all this time, around them, without my help."

"What about Knox?" Major asked. "You ain't got no loyalty to him? Even though you know that bitch took his life?"

"I believe it was an accident."

"Then you a fucking fool."

"If ever the day comes where I feel like she sincerely lied to me, make no mistake I will—"

"What?" Major interjected. "Kiss her to death? Fuck her brains out? Exactly what will you do to avenge our brother's death you turn coat ass, nigga?"

Slade groaned. "Nothing you can say will rattle me, man. My mind is made up."

"Then why the fuck you tell me?" He roared. "Why not just bounce and save some fucking time?"

"Because we blood. And I wanted to eye you face to face like a man."

Major shook his head. "And Memory? Your kid's mother?" He paused. "Guess you don't give a fuck about her though. 'Cause she ain't sucking blood like that red bitch back in the city."

"We were hoping you'd look after her," Killa said. "To make sure she good."

"Just until we get back," Audio added.

Major looked at the two of them and laughed. "Wow, this nigga really convinced ya'll to go hunting for this blood sucking, scandalous bitch. At least he fucking her. What's in it for ya'll, niggas?"

"Easy, bruh!" Slade roared before taking a deep breath. "You may not like her but she's mine all the same."

Major peered in his direction before standing up slowly. "If the three of you go back to D.C. every last one of ya'll dead to me. That's on mama's grave."

Audio leaped up and tried to touch him, to reason with him like family. "Come on, man! We brothers."

Major pushed him with a flat palm to the chest and shook his head. "Have you ever stopped to think that these mothafuckas might be crazier than you think?" He paused. "Nobody knows who they really are, Slade. Or where they came from. And you really ready to risk it all?'

Slade looked un-phased. "Fuck it. It's your life. Have at it playa, playa." He stormed off.

CHAPTER FIVE

THE FOLD

THE PAST

"He killing innocent bystanders. And I'm not about to catch a bullet because of you."

*T*he men were made large with the kind of muscularity you get from sustained effort in prison. And now in charge of a few patients, they were also partially responsible for raping some of the women, which was bound to put a dark light on the mental institution the bosses weren't willing to suffer. And now under the cover of night, on their knees in the soft dirt behind Crescent Falls, the patients were waiting on the call for their lives to be snuffed out.

It was winter.

And the cold air ripped through the thin hospital gowns they wore as if they were naked. Adding to their discomfort the orderlies had instructed them to keep their fingers on their heads causing their muscles to buckle.

"Can I stand up?" Laverne asked, her body trembling from discomfort and the icy weather. "I'm a little older than the rest and my knees are throbbing."

"Oh...so you want to get up huh?" Inmate O asked. "You're having a hard time?"

She nodded, believing he understood. "Yes…the pain is unbearable."

He smiled. "You poor, poor baby." Slowly he walked up to her and struck her on the side of the face with the butt of the gun. Lewis leapt up, preparing to charge him when Inmate O shot one of the other patients who were kneeling in the head, in a show of defiance. This murder stopped Lewis cold and also dropped their numbers to twenty-two.

"Now, I could've killed you but I wanted you to see what happens when you disobey the rules." Inmate O smiled at Lewis. "You still wanna step to me? Or are you coming to your senses?"

Lewis glared and lowered himself to the ground slowly, between Morton and Porter. Laverne looked on in disbelief. "Happy now, nigga?" Porter asked through clenched teeth while the three inmates talked amongst themselves. "You getting niggas off'd. Fuck wrong with you, kid?"

"At least I tried," Lewis whispered. "That's better than I can say for you."

"Except now you got somebody killed."

"Don't be a punk. They gonna kill us anyway if we do nothing."

"They gonna rape me again," Courtney wept, each heavy breath making it obvious that she was on the verge of a

panic attack. "I can feel it! Please...please. I...I'm gonna be sick. I'm...I'm gonna throw up."

"Shut...up...bitch," Morton whispered. "You saw what just happened. He ain't killing the niggas that act up." He looked over at the corpse on the ground, her blood seeping into the earth. "He killing innocent bystanders. And I'm not about to catch a bullet because of you."

The back door suddenly opened and the director, a pale white woman with carrot orange hair walked out, her yellowing smile exposing her ugly personality. She was all evil, no love. "Don't be afraid people," Dr. Mistral said to the patients. "All of this will be over soon. Trust me."

"What's going on?" Lewis asked her. "I mean, why...why are we out here? We got rights you know! It's freezing and ya'll won't even give us coats."

She smiled again. "You're out here because you're waiting."

"On what?"

"An eighteen wheeler."

He looked at everyone in confusion and then back at her. "What's that for?"

"Your bodies," She grinned before walking back inside.

CHAPTER SIX

BONES

"Say it! Who is more powerful?

Bones walked toward the bar within the mansion with Zashay along his side. Moments earlier Dr. Weil met with each member to go over their health plan and summoned Bones too.

"I know you have a lot going on but we have to do something about that little girl," Zashay told him. "Gregory and Swanson are looking at her differently. I'm afraid for her body and her life." Zashay scratched her scalp.

"Don't worry, they know how to hold back."

"Bones, before Gregory was in Crescent Falls he raped twenty women. Sadistically. You know that! And now with Dr. Weil being low on medication I'm afraid they may do something worse to her."

He laughed. "She should've thought about that before she came here." He looked over at her. "Did you know Mooney wrote in the book about how we hunt? And how we get money?"

"You read the entire thing?"

"No."

"Is there anything in there about Farah?"

He frowned. "Not a lot. Just that she loved dude. But I knew that already. And the nigga dead anyway so who cares." He sighed. "I mean, what is it about me? Why doesn't she look at me like she looked at him?" He paused. "I mean sometimes I feel like cracking her neck to make her love me. It's just that I can't live without her."

Zashay saw the look in his eyes before and knew he was on the verge of losing his mind. Immediately she realized he probably hadn't taken his medicine either because Dr. Weil said the prescriptions were dwindling lately. The meetings for the day were to come up with a new plan for treating their mental health issues and everyone had attended but Bones, who was still salty about how he treated him earlier in his office.

"You can't avoid him forever," Zashay warned, ignoring his question about Farah.

They walked into the bar where a 27-year-old topless Giver/bartender with skin the color of caramel was waiting to serve eagerly. Her titties bounced every time she moved. They vetted her when hunt season was on some years back and she loved giving blood and servicing so much that she begged them to stay.

After a unanimous vote she was invited for a trial period and so far so good.

"Two shots of vodka," Zashay told the pretty girl as she quickly fetched the order. Turning her attention back to Bones Zashay said, "But did you hear me earlier? You can't avoid him forever? Dr. Weil makes sure we don't all go mad and—"

"How has Farah been acting in your opinion?"

Zashay's jaw twitched with slight irritation.

Over the years she had grown to love Farah but there was no denying that Zashay's heart had been and would always belong to Bones. So talking about another woman was the last thing she wanted, even if it was about somebody she respected. "I don't follow your question."

"If you never knew me, and met me later, would you want me?"

Zashay laughed. "You're asking the woman who has been hopelessly in love with you forever? Are you serious?"

Silence.

Zashay grabbed one of the shots of vodka that had been colored blood red due to dye the bartender placed inside the glass. It was the way The Fold liked it and she aimed to please.

"When are you gonna answer my question?" he continued.

She sighed. "You're weak." She blurted out trying to keep it one hundred.

She moved to swallow her drink and he smacked it out of her hand. The shot glass shattered on the floor, cutting her lip lightly. The bartender swept it up expeditiously. "Fuck you just say to me?" He roared. "Because I must be hearing things."

Heavy breaths tightened her chest. "I'm...I'm sorry."

The Bartender placed another drink on the counter for Zashay.

"I might be many things." He paused, taking her drink. "But weak was never one of them." He swallowed it and slammed the glass down. "Never forget that!"

She adjusted in her seat. "I misspoke so let me answer you properly. I didn't know Farah before she came to stay with us but I do know she's accustomed to men who can, well, get what they want when they want."

"And I don't?" His nostrils flared.

"Yes...but she hasn't seen that recently." She paused. "She's bored. And we don't hunt anymore which means we're drinking from the same Givers and — "

"Another!" Bones yelled to the bartender, interrupting Zashay all together. His rage was bubbling at the surface and it was a further example about how not having treatment could make them all lose reason.

"S...sure. Right away." The bartender quickly fetched his order.

"She has never met a man more powerful than me," Bones said pointing at Zashay with his index finger. "Not even that nigga Slade Mayoni and Carlton killed. I'm not even understanding how she could still be in love with a dead man."

"True, but you can't tell her you're powerful. You must show her."

"You know what...you're right." Suddenly he popped up and rushed down the hall with Zashay on his heels. "Wait, what you 'bout to do?" She asked.

He was silent as he marched down the corridor like a man on a mission. When he happened upon Dr. Weil's door Zashay's knees buckled and her jaw hung low. She'd given him advice, true, but the last thing she wanted was for him to give Dr. Weil a piece of his mind, which he'd been threatening to do for the longest.

Without knocking, Bones yanked the door open and stood before Dr. Weil who was typing on his laptop vigorously. Dr. Weil looked up at him once, to see who was there before focusing back on his keyboard. "About time. At first I thought you were gonna once again piss me off. I'm so sick of your insolence. When we have a time scheduled I expect you to honor it or—"

Bones raised his .45, which he kept on him at all times, and pulled the trigger. Dr. Weil's brains splattered on the wall behind him, his life snuffed out instantly.

He didn't even see what hit him.

Standing in the doorway, Zashay dropped to her knees in disbelief. Her heart pounded at the walls of her chest plate, making her feel like she was on the verge of a panic attack. Which was something that had plagued her all her life. "Bones...what have you done?" Her question was barely above a whisper. "What have you done to all of us?"

He walked up to her, barrel still hot. "Now who's more powerful?"

"Bones—"

"SAY IT! WHO IS MORE POWERFUL?"

"You are," she cried.

He looked down at her and walked calmly away.

It may have appeared that they were the only two present, but another person also witnessed the assassination and took to urinating where she stood.

FARAH

Cutie zipped into Farah's room where she stood in front of the mirror combing through her hair with her fingers. When she saw the anxious teen in her private quarters she turned around. Cutie's long black hair was plastered to her warm ivory colored skin that was splotched with what looked like smeared red kisses. "What's wrong with you?" Farah asked. "And why your jeans wet?" Farah adjusted her boobs in the long silky black dress she was wearing to make sure they sat right. "Wait...did you pee on yourself?"

"Where my mother?" Cutie asked closing and locking the door behind herself.

"Your mother? Really?" Farah seemed to float toward her. "You wanted to be here, now you'll be forced to stay. Besides, it's out of my hands."

"But I want to go home." Cutie's body trembled. "*Please.*"

"I told you once you came through those doors you would regret it. Now that time has arrived." Farah looked at her again and realized something was deathly wrong. She grabbed her hand and yanked her toward the bed, away from the door. "But what has you shook? What did you see? Tell me."

"He...he killed him." Cutie pointed at the door. "Bones."

Farah frowned. "Wait...what? Killed who?"

"The man in the office. Bones killed the man in the office."

Farah looked at her long and hard and then all became clear. The one man Cutie feared above all others in the mansion was Bones and the only man who Farah could imagine him killing was Dr. Weil.

Still, could Bones be that foolish?

Knowing the crazies who would lose control within The Fold without Dr. Weil's care.

"I'm scared," Cutie wept. "I'm so scared."

Farah grabbed her shoulders. "It's too late for all that. You must calm down and tell me everything you saw."

CHAPTER SEVEN

SLADE

"Never say no shit like that to me again."

Slade, Audio and Killa were putting the last suitcases in his truck preparing to make the hike all the way from Mississippi to D.C. to find Farah. Mentally he wasn't ready for the trip but nothing was going to stop him from getting her back or at least trying.

That one thing he knew for sure.

It had been a long night trying to explain to Memory that he would be back as soon as possible; even though her spirit told her she was losing him forever. All he wanted to do in that moment was get on the road, and try to piece back a part of his life he knew he couldn't live without.

Nothing else mattered.

Audio approached Slade. "That's the last bag, man. I'ma go get the rest of the beer out your fridge for the ride so we can—"

Suddenly Audio looked as if he'd seen six ghosts and Killa who stood next to him looked equally shook. Slowly Slade turned around to see what had frightened his brothers. The moment he did he wish he hadn't. Outside, his now nine-month-old pregnant baby mother stood in a red lace panty and bra set, a butcher knife clutched in her palm, hovering over her protruding belly.

Slade tried to swallow the lump he felt forming in his throat but it wouldn't go away. "Bae," He approached her slowly. "What...what you doing out here? Without clothes?" He looked around to see who was watching and for the moment it was only his brothers.

But that was a fucking 'nuff.

"Stay right there!" She yelled, forcing him still, blade now aimed in his direction. "Don't fucking come near me." Tears rolled down her cheeks. "I just want you to listen. Just listen to me for one fucking second."

"But what's going on, ma?" Killa interjected. He was trying to be calm but his voice resembled a two year old who had shit his pamper and wanted a rapid change. "Slade gonna be right back. We just got to make a trip for a week or so that's all, mama."

"Shut up!" She pointed at him with the knife. "All you Bakers are a bunch of fucking liars and you know it!"

Killa's hands shot up in the air as if a gun was aimed at him. "You got it. We ain't saying nothing else. Speak your talk."

Memory focused back on Slade. "For the past year and a half I have been everything to you. I was quiet when you wanted, thinking your last girl was too loud or to opinionated because you hated talking about her so much. I kept a clean house. A clean body and even cooked for you and your fucking brothers almost every night! And never, not once, did I turn you down for sex even when I had knee surgery and could barely hold my legs open for you to enter my body without being in severe pain."

Slade looked around and back at her. "And I know that, bae." He looked at the knife again. "But I gotta check on my nephew in D.C." He paused. "I told you that. Killa ain't seen him in a while and —"

"You think I'm fucking dumb?!" She screamed. "You think I'm stupid enough to believe it takes three Bakers to find one kid?" She moved toward Slade and he backed up, seconds before Audio and Killa covered Slade with their bodies.

"Bruh," Audio said to Slade, with eyes still on her, "She fam and everything, but I'ma knock her ass out if she try and stab you! I'm not fucking 'round out here."

"No you won't," Slade demanded, pushing his brothers aside and stepping toward her. "You not gonna do that because she not gonna hurt me." His eyes pled with her to be cool but her stare said she meant murder. "Ain't that right, bae? You not trying to hurt me right? Let my brothers know because they ain't feeling this scene right now."

She nodded; long streams of tears rolling down her face. "You right. I could never hurt you because I love you too much. But that ain't gonna stop be from fucking up this kid inside my body. If you don't want me! You don't want us!" With that she took the knife to her belly and stabbed at her womb. Blood gushed all over the concrete and Audio's sneakers.

Slade rushed toward her. "NOOOOOOOOOO!"

The soft beeping of the breathing machine woke Memory up. Fully rested, she yawned loudly, opened her eyes and rolled her head to the left, where Slade was standing at her side, gawking at her. "Why you do that?" He asked sincerely. "Why would you try to kill what's mine? Knowing how I'd react?"

She glared. "What's yours? What about me?" She paused. "I mean, is that all you're worried about? This fucking baby?"

He stared at her, as if seeing her for the first time. Suddenly she wasn't as beautiful as he recalled. "Are you a lunatic? Is that what you saying? I made a kid with a lunatic and didn't know it until today?"

She swallowed the dry taste in her mouth and attempted to soften her gaze. She let her cuckoo out the clock and was trying to smash that bitch back inside but it wasn't working. "Of course I'm not crazy. You know me better than that." She smiled brighter and took a deep breath. "Guess I over reacted huh?"

Silence

"I wanted you to stay, Slade. I wanted you to be with me and I was willing to do whatever it took." She smiled. "And it must've worked because you still here."

He scratched his chocolate baldhead. *God, please stop me from strangling this chick.* He thought to himself.

"Slade…is, I mean, is our baby okay?"

He sighed deeply, his patience running thin. "He's alive. But you almost cut off his face."

She smiled brightly, very awkwardly for the moment. "Aww…" a single tear traipsed down her cheek. "It's a boy. I always wanted a boy."

"Yeah. It's a boy."

"You know something, when I was ten years old I met my father for the first time." She looked up at the ceiling. "Did I ever tell you that?"

"To be honest, right now, I don't even give a fuck."

"Well I did meet him back then," she continued. "He was so fine too, Slade. Skin like yours and almost just as attractive. You got him beat though in the looks department I can't lie." She giggled. "Anyway, he bought me anything I wanted. All I had to do is say the word and it was done. That's what he used to say too. *'Say the word, Memory and it's done'.* " She took a deep breath that seemed to hold a little longer in her chest. "And guess what else he did for me? He raped me from the point I met him up until my mama caught him on top of me in the back of the red Cadillac he bought her for Christmas. That was the same day my mother killed me."

"Killed you? I don't get it."

"She told me I was dead to her so it was like she murdered me that day. Blamed me for everything.

Even threw me out on the streets. Like it was my fault I was raped."

Slade sat in the chair next to the bed. "What the fuck?"

"I know…sounds as crazy as it really was."

"I'm trying to figure out what I got to do with something like that?" He glared. "I would never take something from you. Definitely not sex."

"The similarities between you and my daddy are so clear and still you don't see 'em." She paused. "I always knew I could never take her place. I'm talking about your ex-girlfriend."

Slade rolled his eyes. This bitch was blowing him.

"I knew there would come a day when you would look for her," she continued. "But I figured I would have a little more time to introduce you to the baby and what a family could be like with the three of us. Maybe then you'd forget her. But you didn't, did you?" She paused. "I wanted that so much that I didn't care what you did to me or how you treated me." She touched his hand. "Just like I didn't care what my daddy took from me. Just as long as he was there."

He snatched away. "That ain't the same thing. "

"But in my heart it is, Slade."

He stood up and paced the room. "If I knew you were incapable of being a mother I would've never—"

"What? Not fucked me? Sucked me? Or let me suck you off?" Spit flew out of her mouth as she spoke. "What the fuck would you not have done, NIGGA!"

"A lady, Memory." He pointed at her. "You know that's what I demand so ain't no need in using that type language."

"Nah, chocolate drop! You demand a woman who will be a placemat for the one you always wanted. Well what about me? What about what I feel and who I want? Don't that count for nothing?"

"Come on—"

"If you leave me, I will hurt your bloodline." She said through clenched teeth. "I promise. I already proved I'm capable."

Slade moved closer to the bed. "Do me a favor, shawty…"

Silence.

"Never say no shit like that to me again." He lowered his head and whispered into her ear. "I've killed men with my bare hands for lesser offenses." He rose up. "You don't know me, Memory. You never did. That's why we could never work."

He stormed into the hallway and ran into Audio and Killa who were waiting on the verdict. Would he have to kill her or nah? "How she doing, man?" Killa asked.

"She tripping."

Audio frowned and looked past his brothers, down the hall. "Wait...what Major doing here? You called him, Slade?"

"Nah."

When they focused on the opposite end of the hallway Major came walking out the elevator and toward them. His head hung heavy. "Is everything cool?" Major asked Slade.

"Yeah, that bitch fine or whatever." Slade shrugged.

Major nodded. "My nephew?"

"He a Baker." Audio said. "You already know the little nigga strong so he made it through surgery okay. She did gash his chin with the knife though, so he'll have a scar for life."

"Fuck!" Major said running his hand down the top of his head. "Trying to mess up a Baker's looks." He sighed. "Listen, Slade, I'm sorry, man. Had I known I would've never done it."

"Done what? This wasn't on you."

"It was." He swallowed. "I told her you were leaving to go chasing behind Farah. And she—"

Audio and Killa were so angry they walked away, while Slade remained, eyes glued on his brother. "So if my son would've died you saying this would be on your head?" He paused. "I mean you that mad that we taking a trip you would turn bitch and get to running your mouth to my kid's mother?"

"Bruh, I made a judgment error, man. You know I ain't mean for none of this to happen."

Slade looked away.

"You wrong as fuck, bruh," Audio said pointing at Major walking back toward him. "Shit could've went a rack of different ways."

"He know it too," Killa frowned.

"Ya'll right and like I said I'm sorry." Major nodded in agreement. "Go handle things with your folks in D.C., Slade." He continued. "I don't want you leaving but I'll see to it that things stay safe down here."

"How I know I can trust you?" Slade glared.

"Because that little nigga in that nursery is family. My family." He placed a hand over his heart. "And 'cause you my brother and I fucked up. Give me a chance to make shit right. Is that a good enough

90   *THE FOLD*

reason?" Slade wiped his hand down his head. "Go see about Farah. I'll be here if you need me. Trust."

When Memory opened her eyes and turned her head Major was at her side reading the newspaper. He folded it, stood up and moved toward her.

"Where is Slade?" She asked.

"He ain't here." Major's tone was quick and short. Definitely to the point.

She rolled her eyes. "So he sent you to watch over me or something? Am I under arrest?" She giggled thinking shit was hilarious. "Ya'll Bakers are something else."

"I sent myself, bitch. And if I even think you got ideas about hurting my nephew again I'ma reveal a side of myself you ain't ever seen." He picked up the paper and sat back down. "Now take your dry ass back to sleep. I'm sick of looking at your face."

CHAPTER EIGHT

THE FOLD

"You wanna play a little before you bounce?"

Cutie walked down the hallway opening every unlocked door in the mansion on a hunt for Melinda. She was ready to leave the property but knew she needed her help first. The last thing she wanted to believe was that she was dead but she was starting to believe that was the case.

Most of the rooms were empty but when she happened upon the eighth door she was in for a rude awakening. Inside were Gregory and Swanson and they both were looking for trouble.

And for them she was prey.

Sipping blood red vodka in black glasses both grinned as if they were given the gift of their dreams.

"Oh, I'm sorry. I was looking for somebody else." She turned to walk out.

"Hold up," Gregory said, gripping his dick. The grossest shit about it was that it was already hard. "You wanna play a little before you bounce?"

When she tried to leave, Swanson leapt up grabbed her hand and shoved her back inside. And when she

THE FOLD

heard the door close and lock, courtesy of Gregory, she farted in her drawers she was so afraid.

"No, I wanna—"

"I heard Mooney told you all our secrets," Gregory said before picking her up and tossing her on the bed like a rag doll. "What she tell you about me though? Say anything about this dick?" He un-fastened his pants, stroked it and crawled toward her. It aimed at her like a knife.

She backed into the headboard. "Please don't do this," she begged.

"Please don't what?" Swanson paused. "Get some of this young pussy? 'Cause if you stay everybody in this house puts out. It's The Fold's way. Why should you be any different?"

"Plus I ain't had a new taste in months," Gregory added, pushing her legs apart. "Why not start with your fine yellow ass?"

"NO! PLEASE DON'T DO THIS! I'M BEGGING YOU!"

Gregory frowned while Swanson waited his turn. "Bitch, fuck all that, you 'bout to take this dick so get ready." Gregory ripped the tights she had on and tore her panties off with one pull. Before long the tip of his penis was waiting at the entry of her vagina, ready to push through. He was almost fully inside until she bit him on the shoulder, tearing into his flesh.

And not in the good Vamp way either. That shit hurt.

"Fuck!" He yelled holding his shoulder.

Partially naked, Cutie hustled off the bed, pulled open the door and ran right into the arms of Farah who was hunting for Bones after learning about Dr. Weil's murder.

"What's going on?" She frowned when Gregory and Swanson ran out, their pants undone. Cutie on the other hand hid her nakedness behind Farah.

"Uh…we were—"

"About to rape a girl," Farah said, cutting Gregory off. "What happened to the rule? Only adult Givers?"

Gregory smiled before glaring at her. "If you don't want that little bitch to get eaten, don't put her on the plate." He shrugged. "That's all I'm saying."

Swanson chuckled. "That's right. Anybody behind these mansion walls get got. You know that."

Farah removed the jacket she was wearing and wrapped it around Cutie's bottom. "Go to my room and stay there."

Cutie took off running, feet slapping against the marble floors.

When she was gone Farah stepped closer to them. It was time to put them in their place. "She's off limits. Stay away from her."

"And if we don't?" Swanson asked. "What the fuck you plan to do?"

Farah grinned at them and walked away.

This can't be happening. This can't be happening. Farah repeated to herself. First she got word that Dr. Weil might be dead and already two serial offenders were showing their true mental issues. Before long she knew it would be the entire house and that scared her to death because Dr. Weil wasn't there to treat them and now they would all pay. Thanks to Bones' careless move.

Farah didn't mind a little crazy.

In fact, she felt comfortable around it. Still, she worked better with organized chaos as opposed to manic behavior.

When she finally spotted Bones outside, she zipped up to him with rage. He was talking to a few members of The Fold as if everything was okay. But she was quite aware it wasn't. Since she'd been to Dr. Weil's office and he wasn't there, she was hoping that Cutie had gotten things all wrong but something felt off the moment she stepped in the office, the stink of death was still in the air. Placing her hand on his arm she said, "Bones, can I talk to you in private?"

He turned around and faced her. Smiling first, he winked at her secondly before addressing his men. "We'll speak more later." They walked off, giving them privacy. "Yes, beautiful?"

Her eyes lowered. "Is it true?"

"Is what true?"

"Bones!" She placed her hands on her hips. "Stop playing with me. Did you kill him?"

He chuckled. "Look, I don't want you to be afraid. I don't want you to fear anything honestly." He touched her face. "Because I'm here and at the end of the day, that's all that matters."

"Bones, do you realize what's going on?" She asked almost out of breath. "Do you realize what you've done? You have placed everybody in this house in fucking danger." She pointed at the mansion. "I just walked in on Gregory and Swanson about to rape

Cutie. Without constant help this house will be hell! Is that what you want?"

He frowned. "First off that kid already got hoe eyes." He pointed at her. "Trust me, she done took some dick before. As far as everybody going crazy don't you think I can take care of you if shit get out of hand?"

"I'm not talking about that!" She yelled, causing a few members congregating on the patio to look their way. "I'm talking about madness! It's gonna get out of hand!"

Embarrassed at her level of disrespect, Bones yanked and dragged her inside, toward his bedroom. They were almost there when she snatched away from him roughly. "Let me go!" Her breath quickened. "I'm not moving another step until you fucking talk to me! Did you kill him? Fucking give me an answer."

Zashay, hearing the noise, but knowing the truth, walked up to them. "Is everything cool with you two? I mean, can I help?"

Bones' glare on Zashay was so intense she regretted even asking.

Ignoring Zashay he focused back on Farah. Nostrils flaring he said, "I told you I have things under control."

"But you killed Dr. Weil! That was so stupid!"

Tiring of the impertinence, Bones backhanded her and she dropped down, her knees stabbed into the black and red marble floor. It had been the second time he hit her for the day and she was growing ill. Immediately her skin broke out in hives, something that hadn't happened in a while.

Seeing the melee, Swanson and Gregory walked up to the scene.

"Look at you," Bones continued, spit flying from his mouth. "Skin splotching up. Hair all over the place. You don't even look good enough to be on my arm. Got the nerve to question me."

Swanson and Gregory chuckled.

"You must learn respect, Farah," Bones continued. "I've allowed you to get away with how you talk to me for far too long." He pointed a long finger her way. "It's gonna stop today."

Farah held onto her bleeding mouth.

"I won't be your punching bag forever, Bones," she said in a whisper. "And when the tables are turned, I want you to remember me here, like this. I want you to play this moment over and over in your mind because it will be the reason you die."

Bones bent down, grabbed the back of her hair and stole her in the center of the face.

"OH MY GOD!" She yelled holding her nose.

"You will be whatever the fuck I want you to be, bitch." He moved to hit her a final time when Zashay, seeing the horror, dropped to the floor and used her body as a shield to protect her friend.

"Please don't hit her again, Bones! She get the picture already." She pleaded. "Look at her. I'm begging you."

Bones rose slowly and glared at Zashay. Immediately her stomach bubbled knowing she angered him more than she intended. Now Mayoni and Carlton also approached the group after hearing from others that something dark was occurring in the mansion.

"Bones, can we help?" Carlton asked looking at Farah.

"Take Farah to the box."

"The box...but...are you sure, man?" Carlton continued. "We ain't used it in awhile and —"

"I'm positive." Bones stared at him coldly. "Take Gregory and Swanson with you."

Gregory and Swanson rubbed their hands together like they were about to eat. "Is she still off limits?"

Gregory questioned. "I don't want to touch her if she is. I prefer to —"

"For twenty four hours, do whatever you want to her." He paused. "But Carlton you make sure she gets there."

Gregory and Swanson were so excited their dicks grew swollen.

"You got it, I'll, I'll take her," Carlton said clearing his throat before helping Farah to her feet.

Zashay stood up and walked up to him, trying to talk some sense into his mind. "Bones, please don't put her there," Zashay pled looking at Gregory and Swanson. Although Gregory was known for his sexual mental appetite, Swanson was a killer and twenty-four hours alone with Farah would be far too much time. At the end of the day the chances of her surviving were slim with those dudes. "You...you know what can happen to her. Please, don't do this."

He smiled, although nothing about his facial expression was friendly. Nodding once, he walked off.

Mayoni grabbed Farah's right arm while Carlton maintained hold of her left. "Bones, talk to me!" Farah yelled as she was dragged away, Gregory and Swanson following. "Bones, please don't do this! I'm begging you!"

Mayoni and Carlton tossed Farah into the Ice Box, which was an all-metal room where they blasted air inside as a means of torture. There was one metal toilet, no bed or linens or items of comfort. When Farah banged into the wall across the door due to being thrown hard, Mayoni pranced up to her while Gregory and Swanson were instructed to wait outside for a little privacy. Carlton, however, remained at her side.

"Wow, this is the moment I've been waiting on forever." Mayoni said to Farah in a sinister tone. "I always told you, if Bones isn't happy, I have no use for you. And that day has come."

Farah charged her. "Dr. Weil is dead! Did he tell you that?"

Mayoni frowned. "Yeah right. Bones would never—"

"I'm telling you the truth! Do you know what will happen to us if we stay here? These people aren't meant to live without care. You know that. You were at Crescent."

"Careful, Farah." She paused. "I am these people you talk about. BE careful. You were always the drama queen."

Before Mayoni could defend herself, Farah grabbed hold of her hair with one hand and banged at her face with a fist with the other. Carlton did all he could to pry Mayoni from Farah's hold and it took several moments before he was successful. When he finally separated them, Mayoni wiped hair and blood from her face and glared at Farah.

"You are officially my only enemy." She paused. "And to think, I thought you loved your brother, sister and Slade. Guess I was wrong and now I'm gonna have to kill all of them."

Farah's eyes widened. "Mayoni!"

"Nah, bitch, don't beg now!" She paused. "Should've thought about that before you got out of hand. Now it's my turn to—"

"You didn't let me finish," Farah interrupted. "Because lets be clear, you are the one who told Bones you killed Slade. So if he's alive that's a lot of explaining to do on your part not mine." She pointed to herself.

Mayoni grinned. "So do you suggest I kill him to keep the lie alive?"

Farah swallowed the knot in her throat, took a deep breath and slid to the cold floor. No way in the world she wanted her man dead. Blood from her nose rested on her upper lip. With her head hung low she said, "Please don't hurt him. Please don't hurt my family either."

"Then I suggest you remember who is in charge. Because even if I kill Slade and his brothers, Bones would never find out because I'd kill you first."

Farah looked down. "Can you leave me alone...please?"

Mayoni grinned and looked out the open door at Gregory and Swanson who were waiting, dicks swollen, tongues hanging out the sides of their mouths. "Oh, sweetheart, the last thing you're going to be is alone." She and Carlton walked out and Gregory and Swanson bopped inside, closing the door behind themselves."

When the door locked Carlton grabbed Mayoni's arm and pulled her a few feet from the room. "You know I have supported you from the gate but this vendetta you have against Farah is gonna cause problems for us." He whispered.

"How you figure? We have the upper hand."

"The worst thing you can do is underestimating a person who has nothing to lose."

"Carlton, look at where she is." She pointed at the closed door. "There is nothing she can do to us. EVER! We are in charge and it's high time she be brought down a level or two."

"She's in a closed room with the worst The Fold has to offer." He paused. "And you could've talked Bones out of it if you would've just tried." He breathed deeply. "If you keep fucking with her I'm sure she'll find away to get even. Don't forget, we liked her because she was already menacing when we met her. Do you really thing because Bones locked her up in a mansion that things have changed?"

She shook her head in disgust. "You used to be a real man. I don't know what happened to you. And still it doesn't even matter." Mayoni paused. "Now go make yourself useful and find out if our contacts still got eyes on the Baker boys. Because everything else you saying is a waste of my time and energy." She rolled her eyes and stormed off.

CHAPTER NINE

THE FOLD

THE PAST

"On my command, we all attack."

*T*he truck the Inmate Orderlies had been waiting on pulled up alongside Crescent Falls and Courtney who spotted it first, was so scared she peed on herself, urine soaking into the soil under her knees, for a brief moment making her warm.

The Inmate Orderlies didn't seem to notice the patients were now on edge because nestled in toasty coats, they happily talked amongst themselves about their plans for Christmas later that evening.

"Fuck." Lewis whispered to Morton. "What now?"

"I don't know, man," he looked at the three Inmate O's who were still heavily engaged in conversation. "But we can't go out like this." He paused. "What you think they gonna do to us anyway?"

Lewis sighed. "I don't know. I'm as clueless as you. But it can't be good."

The inmate orderlies finally noticed the parked 18-wheeler that pulled up and grinned. Turning to the patients

Inmate O1 said, "Looks like your ride is here. Won't be much longer now."

"Please! I'm begging you not to – " One of the patient's sentence was shortened when he shot her in the chest for no reason.

All of the other patients screamed and he shot four more, reloaded and shot four more when they were about to scurry just for fun. "Back on your knees! NOW OR I'LL PUT A BULLET IN ALL YOUR HEADS!" He yelled. When the rest were back down, hands on top of their heads as demanded, he calmed down. "I'm not gonna tell you the same thing again. I'm in charge, not the other way around."

Suddenly Inmate O2 sniffed the air. "Hold up...you smell that?" He asked Inmate O1.

Inmate O1 sniffed hard too. "Yeah." He paused. "It's smoke or a barbeque. But where is it coming from?"

Inmate O2 looked at the building. "I don't know but I'm going to find out." He disappeared inside.

"I'm going too," Inmate O3 said. "You got 'em right? I don't want that crazed director bitch coming out and going off because you don't have anything under control." He chuckled. "You done already killed enough of 'em."

"Yeah, sure," Inmate O1 raised his weapon on the remaining thirteen. "I think by now they know we not fucking around."

THE FOLD

When they disappeared inside, grey smoked steamed from one of the windows on the building an Inmate O1 was so curious he focused all of his attention on the scene instead of his hostages. "What the fuck is going on?" He said to himself.

The patients used this time to speak amongst themselves.

"Listen, if we don't move now we won't live to regret it," Lewis whispered.

"I agree," Laverne said in a hushed tone. "It's now or never."

When Courtney looked at each patient dead on the ground her forehead began to sweat despite it being chilly. "Don't do it," she said to them. "Or I'll – "

Giovanna slammed her hand over Courtney's mouth and whispered into her ear. "I will snap your fucking neck if you say one thing. I promise." She paused. "Now put your hands back on your head and shut the fuck up."

Slowly Giovanna placed her hands back on her own head. Courtney quickly obeyed and Inmate O1 didn't see anything.

Lewis winked at Giovanna, loving her style. "Now...on my command," he said, "We all attack."

CHAPTER TEN

SLADE

"Follow my instructions to a T and shit will be sweet."

The night sky covered Slade's SUV as he drove down a dark road leading to D.C. Every so often his eyes would close due to being sleepy before flying open when he heard his tires rolling over the rumble strips along the road. Audio and Killa were so afraid that they'd each take brief naps because somebody had to be sure that Slade didn't kill them all in a car accident.

"I wish you let me push this joint, man," Killa yawned from the backseat. "You gonna get us dead before we get there." He stretched his arms and scratched his head.

Slade looked at his face from the rear view mirror. "Why should I hand over the keys? So you can crash my ride too?" He chuckled. "Like you did that Benz you had for two hours? Nah, bruh, I'm good."

"Well what about me?" Audio asked tucking his phone into his pocket after scrolling The Gram for hours. "I can—"

THE FOLD

"Nah, man," Slade said shaking his head briskly from left to right. "Ain't happening. Don't even ask again."

"But why not?"

"'Cause you drive too fucking fast for one. And for two—"

"Slade, you gotta start trusting me a little," Audio pleaded. "I know I'm younger but I'm still a man."

Slade looked at Killa in the back seat and they both broke out into heavy laughter. This nigga was comedy at best.

"Fuck so funny?" Audio asked.

"Where you want me to start?" Slade said.

"Look, I can drive, Slade," Audio continued. "Pull over and let me prove it."

Slade thought about the offer and checked in with his body condition. With Memory trying to stab at his seed, fussing with her all night and wanting to get at Farah, he wasn't in the best frame of mind. Add to his troubles he was physically exhausted. They had a long hike from the south and he knew he wouldn't make it since he didn't want to bunk down at any hotels in Mississippi, for fear The Fold would make good on their promises to kill them. No, if he wanted to get there, he needed to rely on his brother's help.

"Okay, man," Slade said in a huff.

Audio slapped his hands together and smiled. "That mean I get to change the radio too right? 'Cause you been playing some bullshit all—"

"Listen," Slade interrupted, his tone serious. "You gotta follow these directions." He handed him a piece of paper that was sitting on his lap. "Take only these back roads and hit the highways only if it's on this sheet. Follow my instructions to a T and shit will be sweet. We gotta be careful out here. Niggas are looking for us."

Audio looked at it and frowned. "Aight, man but it'll take us forever to get there with—"

"DID YOU HEAR WHAT I FUCKING SAID?" Slade yelled. "DON'T TAKE A HIGHWAY UNTIL YOU SEE IT HERE! I MAPPED IT ALL OUT! ALL YOU GOTTA DO IS FOLLOW FUCKING DIRECTIONS!"

Audio's eyes widened. "Okayyyyyyyyyy, man! You ain't gotta be spitting in my face and shit. We gonna be good, trust me."

Slade's instincts said not to hand over the wheel but what could he do? He needed the break and Killa was good and terrible when it came to driving. For the moment Audio was the lesser of two bad drivers so he would have to take the bait.

Five minutes later Audio had the wheel and surprisingly Slade and Killa felt comfortable enough with his driving flow to drift off to sleep. Low key the only reason Audio wanted to drive was because he who controlled the wheel regulated the music. And although loud, Slade and Killa didn't mind what he was playing because the break was necessary for them both.

Two hours later Slade woke up in the passenger seat and noticed Audio was on the highway rapping along to a Kendrick Lamar song. Confused, he wiped his eyes, snatched the sheet out of Audio's lap and looked at his watch. "Hold up, you on the highway already?"

Audio sighed deeply. "Come on, man, we fine. I done saved time and everything, plus nobody's tailing us."

Slade's nose flared as he looked around to be sure they weren't being followed. "Get off on the exit." His tone was calm but his expression said murder.

"Why though? I still got some energy in me."

"Do what I fucking say!" Audio shrugged and did as he was told. When he parked Slade said, "Now get out."

"Fuck it, you drive then. I was just trying to do you a favor." Audio said opening the door, easing out and moving toward the passenger side. But before Audio could ease back into the confines of the truck, Slade was right behind him to deliver a blow to the belly.

Audio, never able to handle his big brother's punches, dropped where he stood. One knee on the ground and a hand on his gut, Audio looked up at Slade barely able to talk let alone breathe. "Fuck you do that for?"

"This why I didn't want you to come!" Slade pointed at him. "You can't take small instructions. What are you? Two years old?"

"But I saved time!"

"I'm not trying to save time." He pointed at the ground. "I'm trying to save our lives."

Finally Audio rose, fingers still on his belly as he hoped the pain would subside. "You making more out of this than you should."

"Nah, you just don't listen. After all this time, you still immature. That's why I didn't want you to come. And you wouldn't be here if you weren't the only one who knows where she lives."

Killa eased out the truck and rubbed his eyes. Looking at how angry Slade was he asked, "So the lil nigga took the highway anyway huh?"

Silence.

"Told you he would though," Killa chuckled once.

The joke was over when suddenly headlights pulled up behind the truck. When the brightness moved closer, they could see the grill of a black Impala and smoked out windows surrounding the vehicle. A tall light skin dude with splotchy hair stepped out and immediately Slade was disgusted with himself that he didn't take his hammer out from up under the front seat. Glancing over at his brothers he could gauge by the looks on their faces that they were also strapless.

"Yah country boys need help?" Splotch Face asked, with his friend Blue Baseball Cap and other friend Bald Head behind him offering muscle.

"Nah, we good," Slade said, nodding a few times.

"I'm glad to hear that," Splotch Face continued, taking one more step closer. "'Cause we hate for you to be bad out here, since we 'bout to take everything you got."

With that Splotchy and his mob pulled out .45's and pointed them at the Bakers. Slade was so angry he contemplated taking a bullet just to get his hands around Splotch Face's neck. But although he held superhero tendencies in his mind, he couldn't say the same for his brothers. And as a result the stick up boys relieved them of their money, truck and luggage.

CHAPTER ELEVEN

BONES

"Isn't it time now that we embrace who we are,

even if it's perceived as evil or violent?"

The Shikar Room was crowded as all members of The Fold, along with some Givers, focused on Bones who was confirming what they already knew.

That Dr. Weil was dead.

A few of the Fold members gasped upon hearing the news but Mayoni, Carlton and Zashay already knew the deal. Some of the members, specifically the new ones inducted, cried.

"Well, what happened?" Nicola asked Bones. "Because this can't be good for us. Right?"

"He had plans to do us like he did the others in Crescent Falls," Bones lied. "Give us some medicine and kill us all. Luckily for all of us I found out about it ahead of time and took the nigga out."

More members gasped.

"He didn't respect us or what we stood for so I'm in charge now." He looked at all of them individually. "And I know most of you are worried, especially the new inductees," Bones continued with Mayoni to his right and Zashay to his left. "But you need to know that I have assisted Dr. Weil in all of his business interactions and we will be okay."

"He's right," Mayoni added. "Dr. Weil didn't do a thing without him. This family is safe with Bones at the helm. Trust me."

"But what about the medicine?" Eve asked. "Or pain therapy?"

"We don't need it anymore!" Bones suggested. "I mean, how do you feel now? Do you feel like you need medication just to live? Just to survive? 'Cause you look okay to me. Isn't it time now that we embrace who we are, even if it's perceived as evil or violent?"

Some members agreed but Zashay, Denny and Wesley didn't seem convinced.

"This is good for us," Bones continued. "Finally we will be able to live without being under the influence of drugs unless it's recreational." He paused. "And to show you that things are going to run smoothly, I am reinstituting Shikar."

Applause erupted in the room and Bones head rose higher as the Bartender walked around with a tray of blood red champagne. With Mayoni's recommendation to bring back the hunt he was instantly a fan with The Fold and that easily he won them over. Although he knew how important medication and pain therapy was, he was certain he wouldn't need any of it.

At least he hoped.

"I will be giving you all details on Shikar and when the next hunt will be," Mayoni said. "Bones has left me in charge and it will prove to be a great event leading up to the ceremony."

"Who will get to go?" Zashay asked. "To the hunt?"

"I'll notify everyone soon so don't worry," Mayoni said, nodding at her. "I have it under control." She felt so proud that Bones was now king.

Bones placed a firm hand on Mayoni's shoulder before accepting a glass from the Bartender. "Now. Let us toast. To The Fold."

Everyone raised their glasses. "To The Fold."

After they drank their champagne the music turned on and everyone celebrated. Slowly Zashay walked up to Bones, her arms folded across her chest. "Can I talk to you for a minute? In private?"

Ten minutes later they were in Dr. Weil's office, his body removed by outside services over an hour ago. And now Bones sat in the man's chair as if it were his the whole time. Maybe in his mind it was. "What is it, Zashay?"

She moved closer to the desk. "I'm afraid for Farah's life." She paused. "You know Gregory and Swanson have the potential to kill her!"

He sighed. "Since when has this bitch meant more to you than me?"

"It's not that. It's just—"

"You know, I've been reading some of the book that little girl brought in here. And I saw a passage about you having sex with her on the outside of this mansion. With some bum ass nigga ya'll killed after drinking blood from his dick. Without my authorization. Is that true?"

She swallowed the lump in her throat because it was correct. But she didn't want him knowing. "No, Bones. I just think she shouldn't be—"

"She told me not to trust you, you know." He grinned.

"No...no she didn't."

He glared. "So you're calling me a liar?"

"No...of course not, but I don't get why she would say that." She paused. "We're...we're not really friends but we're cool and it doesn't make any sense."

His brows lowered. "She said you a conniving bitch," he continued to lie. "And that all you want is to hurt me. You got me thinking maybe she's right the way you acting."

Zashay flopped in the seat. "I don't understand. Why...why would she say those things?" Her head hung low upon hearing the evil words.

Bones stood up, walked around the front of his desk and sat on the edge. "Don't look so hard. Farah is charming. That's why I fell for her. But at the end of the day she is still a liar and she did tell me not to trust you."

"But I thought she —"

"What? Was your friend?" He laughed. "She's only concerned for herself."

She nodded yes.

"Soon you'll realize something, Zashay." He walked over to her and raised her chin. "The only one who truly cares about you in this world is me. Forever and always."

She rose up, walked across the room and stood in the corner. With her arms wrapped tightly around her own body she slowly looked into his eyes, wanting to believe him so desperately. But if anything time had showed her that Bones could be fickle and moody so she got over trying to be the only one he truly cared about. "You don't give a fuck about me. And you know it."

He walked over to her, slipped his arms around her waist and stared at her for a moment. "Oh yeah? Well tell me why I want you to be my wife? Explain that shit to me."

Zashay's legs buckled and she could barely stand. She felt like she was hearing things. "Your wife?"

He smiled. "You gonna make me ask twice?"

"But...you can't stand me."

He chuckled. "That's where you're wrong. If I felt that way you wouldn't be alive. I got the world now, Z. I'm leader of the most powerful secret organization. And do you know what that means? Nothing if I don't have a rider at my side." He nodded at her. "I want that to be you. The question is, are you worthy and ready?"

She walked away and he followed. All of her life she wanted to hear those words but now, now they seemed unreal. Or was it her mind playing tricks on her already? Without Dr. Weil's care anything was possible that was certain.

"I'm waiting..."

"I want this. You know I do."

He grinned and approached her again. "Then why don't you seem happy?" He turned her around so they could face one another.

"You have a way of giving me the world and then leaving me homeless, Bones. So I don't want to be excited if this isn't going to be real in the morning."

He laughed. "Be happy."

"Bones, I'm serious! I don't want to fall in love with you again, only for you to let go." She continued. "So if you're playing games I beg you not to do this to me. I can't take another...another heartbreak. Not without Dr. Weil's care."

"Look, stop saying that nigga's name. He's dead and I'm in charge. Now I want you as my wife," he paused. "The only thing you need to do now is say yes or no."

"Yes, Bones," she smiled grabbing his face with both hands. "Of course I want to be your wife. You know I do. I've wanted nothing more for so long."

They kissed passionately before he turned her around. Removing his gold razor from his pocket, he nicked her on the shoulder and suckled the blood oozing from her skin. As she moaned he took off her shirt and pants and smiled.

"Damn, you sexy," he complimented. Zashay had always kept her body right and he was proud to see that this time was no different.

Wanting to go to the next level, he took off her white bra and panty set before looking at her briefly once more. Then he lowered down, sliced into the flesh of her left butt cheek and ran his glistening wet tongue over the liquid and moaned. "Sweet." Inhaling the delicious smell of her pussy he rose, removed his dick and stroked it once since it was already stiff. "Touch your toes, I wanna see that thing open wide." She placed her fingers on her feet and bent forward as commanded. With her pussy spread he pressed into her and she bit into her bottom lip. "Damn, shawty," he moaned.

She juiced up even more when she heard how he responded to her. "Damn I miss you inside of me. You won't make a mistake, Bones by choosing me. I promise."

"I know I didn't. But now it's gonna be forever," he said, pumping a few more times before he came on top of her ass cheek, a clumpy white mess on her flesh, just that fast he was done with her. "That shit was official!" He grabbed the same towel Dr. Weil tossed in his face off the desk and said, "Clean up."

"Okay."

She grinned, wiped her ass and put back on her clothes. He walked up to her and said, "Now that we've made things official I need something from you." He paused. "When Gregory and Swanson are done with Farah I want you to let her know that you are my new woman."

She nodded. "Of...of course, Bones."

"I mean physically. Basically I want you to beat her ass."

THE FOLD
THE PAST

Things were heating up as Lewis, the self-proclaimed leader tried to contemplate the perfect moment to charge Inmate O1. When he felt it was time he looked over at Morton and nodded.

"Kill!" He yelled.

Inmate O1 was so caught off guard at the group of mad men charging him that he fumbled with the gun. Not being able to regain control, Lewis knocked it out of his hand and all thirteen beat him senseless. Once on the ground the patients kicked, bit and scratched his body causing him extreme pain from every pore of his skin. But it was the boot to the head by Porter that caused his brain to knock against his skull and kill him instantly.

Just then the back door came flying open and with it a stronger odor of smoke. Dr. Weil's honey brown face was wet with sweat as he looked frantically at the bunch, while orange flames blasting from behind let all know that the building was engulfed in flames.

Next, glancing down at the other bodies of patients he was angry that he hadn't come sooner. The door slammed shut. They were about to kill him too until he yelled, "Stop!" His palms in their direction.

"Why should we not kill you too?" Lewis yelled, heaving breaths as they contemplated pummeling him.

"Yeah!" Porter added. "'Cause we ain't letting nobody off us like they did them." He looked at the bodies in the grass.

"Because I got the keys to that truck," he dangled them and nodded toward the eighteen-wheeler. "And I'm also the one who set this place on fire. Not only can you trust me you need to know I'm on your team."

The thirteen sat on a pile of uniforms in the back of the trailer, Dr. Weil, a part of them. Although they trusted him somewhat for the moment, they still didn't know what he wanted from them. After all, why was he so kind?

One of Dr. Weil's friends drove the 18-wheeler away from the flaming institution as they spoke in the back.

Dr. Weil cleared his throat. "I am — "

"We know who you are," Lewis said, interrupting him. "What we don't know is what you want from us. We ain't got shit."

"Nothing." Dr. Weil said. "I mean…all I want is to help you."

They snickered. "You mean by raping us?" Courtney asked. "Like everyone else did back in that place!"

Have I ever touched you inappropriately?" Dr. Weil questioned. "Just once, Courtney?"

She looked away, surprised he knew her name.

"That ain't the fucking point." Lewis said. "Everybody in Crescent been grimy!" He yelled. "Why should you be any different?"

Dr. Weil looked downward. "The institution wasn't supposed to be like that. Crescent Falls used to be a good place, which is why I wanted to work for them. I could've gone anywhere but I chose to work there, thinking I could help."

"We already know you're rich, doctor," Laverne grinned. "Done already told them you don't need the money."

Embarrassed, he cleared his throat again. "Thank...thank you, Laverne. Like I was saying it used to be a good place. And then they let in prisoners on a work release program for a few construction and clean up projects when they were adding a new wing. Things were fine until Amanda, the director's secretary, didn't check the records of one inmate who happened to be a level 3-sex offender. Because they were getting work for cheap. And then he raped – "

"Me," Courtney interrupted. "He fucking raped me!"

"Yes, and I'm so sorry about that." Dr. Weil nodded. "For some reason he got away with it which only encouraged a few others with bad motives to take advantage of the situation. I mean, not all the orderlies were like that. In fact, some inmates left who were not like the others but a few stayed and continued on with their evil ways." He paused.

"After awhile things grew worse and a few men were also sexually assaulted."

Porter moved uneasily, having been the victim of one such act.

"I tried to bring it to a few of the director's attention but no one cared. It wasn't until I helped a patient escape recently and she filed a lawsuit that they woke up to what was happening. But instead of facing it, they decided it would be best to get rid of everyone. With a bullet to the head. And thinking I would be off work, they decided to do it on Christmas."

"So how were they going to explain all of us being dead?" Lewis asked.

"I heard it was going to be mass suicide. Put off on one of the patients." He paused. "But I learned about it and put some of the patients to permanent sleep via IV and you — well, I believe there is a future."

"I still don't trust you." Morton said.

"And I understand why you shouldn't." Dr. Weil said. "Except this one thing."

"And what's that?" Morton said.

"I'm all you got."

CHAPTER TWELVE

SLADE

"I can't believe this shit! What we gonna do now?"

Slade, Killa and Audio walked down the dark road, mad as fuck at the world. And Slade didn't know who to be angrier with. Audio for not sticking to the driving instructions he laid out prior to handing over the keys, or himself for ordering him out of the car, which resulted in the roadside robbery.

So they trekked in the darkness on foot without a plan.

"Uh, what we gonna do now?" Audio asked. "'Cause my back—"

"Shut your bitch ass up!" Slade yelled. "I don't give a fuck about your back?"

"How come you mad at me when you the one who got us ganked?" Audio asked.

Slade was about to strike him again until Killa blocked him. "If you hit him again he'll fold over." He extended his hand to stop him. "That's enough for one day don't you think? We already know the little nigga don't listen."

THE FOLD

Slade took an about face and yelled. "FUCK!" He paused. "I can't believe this shit! What we gonna do now?"

They were still kicking country rocks until a white pickup four seater pulled up on them. Slade placed his hand on his waist out of habit but clearly he wasn't strapped so it didn't matter. When a window rolled down the scent of expensive perfume oozed out the car and into the Baker Brothers' nostrils. Taking a peek inside from a far, they saw a woman wearing a white bikini top and stylish blue jeans smiling back at them.

"You fellas need a ride?" She asked. "Or some smoke?" She raised a lit blunt.

Slade took one look at her white skin and smelled trouble. "Fuck no. Keep it moving, pink thing." He shook his head. "Come on, ya'll let's bounce."

Killa grabbed Slade's arm and moved him a little from the car. "Come on, man," he whispered. "These Foamposites killing my bunions. I can't kick no more rocks tonight I swear to God."

When Slade looked at the truck he wanted to hit Audio again after seeing him on the driver's side window talking to the beautiful girl inside. He was being thirsty as fuck and Slade's pressure rose due to his insolence. "Man, this don't feel right. I mean look at that broad. She a ten! How you gonna pull up on three country niggas with no fear unless you the devil himself?"

Killa looked back at her and then his brother. "You right. But we ain't got no options right now, Slade. So in my mind she a come up." He paused. "We can't even get a hold of Major 'cause we ain't got no cell phones. And even if he could send us money we don't have our I.D.'s. Plus you know Major can't leave ole girl by herself to bring paper to us. She'd be liable to hurt neph' again and I know you don't want that. She said it."

Slade sighed. "Nah, I don't even want to tell him what's going on. All he gonna do is say I told you so." He took a long breath. "Aight...so we'll see what's up with her." He pointed at Killa. "But if this bitch get wild I'm killing her with my own hands and you know I can."

Slowly they walked up to the truck and looked inside. "So you fellas gonna let me help you or not?" She asked Slade and Killa.

Slade looked at his brothers and with that they eased in the truck, Audio in the front seat of course.

"I take that as a yes," she smiled tapping the steering wheel once. "So, what happened to you fellas anyway?" She paused as she drove down the street. "Your tires blew out or something?"

"Worse than that," Audio said. "We were robbed."

She placed her hand over her trembling lips and Slade believed she was a good actress. "Are you serious? I'm so sorry to hear that."

"Yeah, them niggas tried to—"

"Audio...you rapping a whole lot right now," Slade said. "How 'bout you shut the fuck up for a second and let the young lady tell us about herself for a change."

"Yeah." Killa confirmed. "We hear you running your mouth all the time."

The pretty driver looked back at Slade and Killa by adjusting her rearview mirror. "I get it. You don't know me." She smiled brighter. "So let's start with a few introductions. Maybe that'll help get the chill out the truck."

"We waiting," Killa said.

"The name's Lilly. But my friends call me Lily." She giggled.

Audio was the only one laughing like she was an episode of Martin.

"So I have a tough crowd," she continued.

"You know of any motels that run real cheap 'round here?" Slade asked.

"Sure…ain't but ten miles up actually. Off I-75N toward Knoxville."

"Take us there."

"Thought you didn't have money." She said playfully.

"We don't." He nodded at her. "You gonna pay for it."

She nodded and looked out the window to her left before looking straight ahead. "I don't mind doing favors. Just as long as when the time comes, the favor is returned."

Slade nodded, sat back and looked at his brothers with the side eye.

She was trouble.

Guaranteed.

Slade, Killa and Audio opened the door to the motel room just as a fat ass rat scurried deeper inside, burying itself in the walls. Slade looked at his younger bros and shook his head at the king bed sitting in the middle of the floor.

"This bitch a garbage bin," Killa said. "YUCK!"

"And I thought we asked for a double," Audio added. "Where we gonna sleep?"

"Yo, bitch ass got the floor," Slade said. "After everything you put me through."

"Yeah right."

Slade ran his hand down his face. "We just gonna have to take it back to the tunnel. When we were kids. Two sleep up one sleep in the middle downward."

"Man, what we gonna do now though? For paper?" Killa asked. "You really don't think we should go home and regroup first?"

"I ain't come all this way without her, man. We going to D.C. no matter what."

Audio flopped on the bed. "Well I'ma see what's up with Lily before —"

"Nah, my nigga, what you gonna do is get your rusty ass in the shower," Slade commanded. "I want you to leave that white girl alone." He pointed at him. "I don't trust her and if you'd use your head you'd know I'm right."

"Why though?" Audio begged, holding his hands in front of him as if he were praying. "She wanna fuck I can feel it."

"White girls fucking niggas ain't new," Slade said. "What is new is one pulling up on three on the side of the road in the middle of the night like its regular. I'm telling you I don't trust her. So until I can make sure she don't get us before we get her, chill the fuck out."

"And what she gonna steal?" Audio continued mad he couldn't smash. "Our jean pockets?"

"NIGGA, AIN'T NOBODY PLAYING WITH YOU!" Slade yelled. "CHILL THE FUCK OUT AND STOP BEING PRESSED!"

Killa walked up to the window, pulled back the filthy doo-doo brown curtains and peered outside. "We definitely can't be here long. I see predators already." He released the curtain and looked at them. "Which means we the prey."

"Just give me until the night to come up with a plan," Slade said. "And lets stick together."

Killa sat on the edge of the bed and removed his shoes. "I never asked bro, guess I really didn't want to know because I'm riding regardless. But what makes her different? What makes her worth all this?"

134   *THE FOLD*

Slade thought about Farah. "She's not afraid of me."

"Huh? How you sound?" Audio said. "We going all the way to D.C. 'cause she ain't afraid of your big ass? What sense that make? Memory look like she can handle you too."

"Women look at me but they don't see me. Farah knows my bad side and she still feeling a nigga. When you get a woman who will take you at your worst you gotta hold on to her."

"This nigga acting like ain't no Mississippi broads would have his ass," Audio said to himself. "Just say you like the redbone and cut the other shit." He shrugged.

Slade shook his head.

"And you'd have her in your life, even if she a monster?" Killa asked.

"We from the same cloth, Killa. For now that's all I can say." Slade paused. "Well I'ma take a shower since neither of you niggas care about being stank. I be back." He walked into the bathroom, closed the door and looked at the toilet.

It was so grimy it stunk .

It was the nastiest place he'd stepped into in ages but being alone in the shower gave him a chance to think about what he was getting himself into. And as he cleaned up he replayed his brother's question repeatedly in his mind.

Was Farah worth it?

Each time he asked himself the answer was yes.

After he showered he left the bathroom only to find Killa sound asleep in the recliner and Audio gone.

"Fuck!"

CHAPTER THIRTEEN

MAYONI

"Contrary to what you believe I don't want to hurt anybody."

Mayoni walked into Cutie's room after getting complaints from the members that she'd been crying for her mother and Farah all night. When she entered Cutie stood up and rushed toward her thinking she was about to be let free. "I couldn't get out." She sniffled. "The door was locked."

"Your point?"

Cutie wiped her tears away. "I want Farah. Where is she?"

Mayoni smiled, grabbed her hair and slapped her face twice. Startled, Cutie ran across the room and leaned against the wall, placing two hands on her mouth to mute her cries. "You don't ask me where anyone is in this house and do you know why?" She walked slowly toward her.

Cutie shook her head no.

"Because you don't belong here." She pointed at her. "The only reason you're still alive is because Bones hasn't given the okay on your murder like he did your mother. But when he does you gone too."

Cutie burst into tears and Mayoni grinned. Finally she knew what Farah said was true, Melinda was dead.

"Now, I'm not gonna keep coming by this room telling you to shut the fuck up. The next thing I do will be permanent so if you enjoy life I suggest you remember that. Am I clear?"

"Yes." Cutie said under her breath. "I'll be quiet."

When Mayoni left the room she locked the door again and turned around, bumping into Carlton on the way out. "What did you say to her?"

"Not much. Just told her to stop all the crying that's all." She shrugged and tried to walk around him but he blocked her steps.

"I heard you."

She frowned. "Then why you ask?"

He grabbed her arm. "You're not gonna hurt that girl." He paused. "I'm not gonna let you."

"Contrary to what you believe I don't want to hurt anybody." She sighed. "The only thing I want is for Bones to be—"

"BONES THIS AND BONES THAT!" He yelled in her face. "What is wrong with you all of a sudden?

What the fuck about me? I'm your nigga! When you gonna start taking into account how I feel?"

"How you sound? I always take into account how you feel, Carlton. But Bones is the leader now and —"

"Wait, you attracted to that nigga, ain't you?" He frowned.

"What? Of course not!" She paused. "That's...that's why I wanted her to be here for him. To make him happy. But now all Farah's doing is breaking his heart."

"Why? Because you wanted to be with him and couldn't?"

"Carlton, cut the dumb shit."

"I'm never gonna stand by and let you have two men." He paused. "At some point you'll have to prove who you're more loyal too. Are you ready for that day?"

She looked at him, rolled her eyes and stomped away.

FARAH

Gregory stood up after he raped Farah for the third time that day. When Bones said he was giving them twenty-four hours, he had intentions on taking her every minute.

Every second.

Swanson, who only needed one taste to get by, sat across the room and enjoyed the scene.

"Damn I missed that juicy pussy," Gregory said to the room. "I can see why Bones was being stingy with you, Farah."

Bloody and covered in semen she peered at him with hate.

"Let me find out after all this she still got some fight in her," Swanson said. "You better be careful, Greg. She might bite that dick off."

"Yeah, but she won't be so strong when I pound that pussy again with my fist," he laughed and clutched his hand. "Ain't that right Farah?"

Suddenly the door to the Ice Box opened and Zashay entered, shaking her head. She was disgusted when she saw Farah's clothes hanging off, her face bruised and bloodied. "Leave me alone with her," she told Gregory and Swanson.

"But Bones said —"

"I SAID LEAVE!" She said screaming in Gregory's face.

He grabbed his shirt and sucked his teeth. "Aight but I be back in an hour. And I'ma remember this shit too." He pointed at her. "Besides, I'm not done with her yet."

When they both exited Farah eased up slowly and walked over to her. "Thank God you're here. Have you seen Cutie? Is she okay? Please watch her because they're going to kill that little girl." She tried to hug her but Zashay took one step backward.

Farah immediately noticed. She was acting different. "Are you okay?"

"Why wouldn't I be?"

"Zashay, please talk to me. You're the only one in here who can help and right now I really need a friend. I really need you. So can you talk to me and tell me what the fuck is up? Why would Bones do this?"

"I'm here ain't I?" She crossed her arms over her chest. "What more you want?"

Farah looked behind her at the door. "Well can you at least tell me if you're here to let me out of this place?"

"You can get out in twenty-four hours when you fall in line, and understand how things work around here." Zashay was stern and this threw Farah for a loop. "Cause things not gonna be the same when you walk out those doors. That's for sure."

Farah took a moment to consider how cold she was being. "Gregory and Swanson have done things to me I don't wanna talk about. My body is throbbing everywhere and I can barely stand up except if I don't, I'm afraid…" she cried a little, "I'm afraid you won't know how much I need your help. Please, Zashay. I need to know if you're still my friend."

"Why should I be your friend?" Her eyebrows rose. "When you talked behind my back about how much you don't like me."

Farah felt queasy. Bones had gotten to her and it worked. "Zashay, don't let him do it." She grabbed both of her hands. "Don't let him tear us apart."

"I don't know what you're talking about."

"We have been so good lately. You gotta know that I've, *never* said anything to Bones about you or any of the things we talked about in private. If he's telling you these things its because he's angry and afraid that you stood up for me earlier. Like I would've done for you." She cried a little more. "Zashay, all I was trying to do is to get Bones to realize how bad it was to kill the doctor. That's it. And now he's making things up!"

"Get over Dr. Weil. Bones is in charge!"

"He's in charge now but it'll be a matter of time before he gets drunk with power and become severely dangerous, Zashay. Dr. Weil wasn't just someone who brought in our money, he was also in charge of the mental health of — "

"You telling me shit I already know! Like you were apart of the original crew."

"Then listen to me!"

"He asked me to be his wife," she interrupted. "And I said yes."

Farah backed away slowly. "Zashay, no, no, no! Don't do this! It's a trap! Don't you see it? He's only using you to get me jealous!"

"Don't do what?" She frowned. "Take your place by his side? Since it's obvious you not feeling him anymore?"

"I'm not feeling him anymore because I don't love him! I never have!" She paused. "If you want my place you can have it but not like this!" Farah walked up to her and touched her shoulders with her chilly fingertips. "Listen, all of my life I have thought about myself. And a lot of people have gotten hurt in the process. This time I'm trying to be something different. I'm trying to put others first. Am I making a mistake?"

"What that got to do with me and my fiancé?"

Farah took a deep breath and shook her head. The chick sounded dumb. "I guess nothing."

Zashay crossed her arms over her chest. "I was supposed to come in here and show you what the new program is by beating your ass. But it looks like Gregory and Swanson already did that so who cares." She paused. "Instead of all the violence I'm giving you a firm warning. Respect Bones. Respect The Fold and respect me. Otherwise you'll have a fucking problem in this house." She stormed out.

Farah walked over to the wall, slid down and wept. "Slade, if you're still alive, wherever you are. Help me. Please!"

CHAPTER FOURTEEN

SLADE

"Let me talk to my brothers first. Alone."

"I know, man." Slade said looking out of the window at the motel. "But I'ma find him, I promise. Anyway I didn't hit you for you to be worrying. Just felt it was only right to let you know what's going on."

"This is why I didn't want ya'll bouncing in the first place. Now you out there with no ID or money?" Major paused. "Let me come get you, man. Stop all this dumb shit, moving around out of town like you don't have family."

"Nah, I'ma make it work," he closed the curtain and walked across the room. The rat that was there earlier didn't even bother to run back in the wall. It just looked at Slade like he was wrong for being in his city. Maybe he was. "Plus now that I think about it, it may be a good thing for us not to have ID's. In case we have to lay some heads. Don't need nobody knowing who we are."

"Well what about paper? 'Cause you can't be rolling broke."

"Like I said, I'll think of something." He sat on the edge of the bed. "I just gotta find Audio first."

Major sighed. "I don't feel good about this."

Slade nodded. "How's my kid?" He was trying to change the topic because at the end of the day he was going to do what he wanted. That part was clear.

"Why? Do you even care about him?"

Slade's nostrils flared.

"Sorry, man," Major continued before Slade even answered. "That was half bitch on my part." He sighed. "It's just that I don't want nothing happening to my brothers. Am I wrong for that?"

"Nah." Suddenly the door opened and Killa rushed inside. "But I'ma hit you back in a second."

"Don't have me waiting long, man. I gotta know about Audio like yesterday."

"I said I got you." Slade hung up and tossed the phone on the bed. "Any word on the streets?"

"A homeless man said he saw Audio and that white broad getting into a cab not too long ago. Said somebody stole her truck from this shithole. He thinks they going to breakfast at a diner a few miles out. Something about Audio being hungry but he actually thought he was being thirsty."

Slade stood up and shook his head. "Let's go find this nigga."

"How we gonna get there?"

"A cab."

Killa frowned. "We ain't got no money."

"And that's gonna stop us how?" Slade tapped him on the shoulder and opened the door. "Let's roll. Shit will work out."

The cab driver pulled in front of a dilapidated building with the words DINER sprawled across the front in neon red letters. The moment the vehicle stopped, Slade opened the car door and eased out.

"Hold up, where my money?" The cab driver asked, frowning.

"I be back with your shit, sit tight." He paused. "Anyway my brother's staying here so you gonna get your fucking money." Slade slammed the door leaving Killa and the driver inside.

Walking into the diner, it wasn't hard to spot his younger brother. For one Audio was being extra loud as he sat in front of Lily at a table in the back of the restaurant. And secondly she was still wearing the same bikini top with jeans she pulled up on them the night before, looking like a slut in a public establishment.

The broad hadn't bothered to wipe her ass.

Slade stomped toward the two, lifted Audio off his feet with one swipe and tossed him on the floor. Next he snatched Lily's pink purse off the table, removed a hundred dollar bill and slammed it back into her lap. All while patrons looked on in horror.

"Get up," Slade told Audio. "We leaving."

Audio rose to his feet, dusted off the back of his pants and waited for the next word from his oldest brother. He knew the look in Slade's eyes was serious and didn't even bother talking back like he had in the past. He really valued life in that moment and wanted to live. They were about to walk away when Lily stood up and said, "Tell him about the money, Audio."

Slade stopped and turned around slowly to face her.

She saw the hungry look in his eyes that said he needed cash like yesterday. "That's right," she continued moving closer to them. "I have a plan that will make you and your brothers close to one hundred

THE FOLD

thousand dollars. And if you got the time, I'd like to share it with you. That is if you're interested."

Slade, Audio, Killa and Lily were sitting in their room going over the plans for the money come up that the Baker boys desperately needed. Lying across the bed behind them were several ripped up bed sheet ropes that Slade had torn.

"So how I know this not a set up?" Slade asked Lily. "Seems awfully convenient you could land this amount of cash."

She laughed. "No disrespect, but set you up for what?" She paused. "You ain't got no money remember? That's why this will work." She pointed at Slade. "But they do."

Killa sighed. "And you sure the payout gonna be that hefty?"

"This card game don't draw thousand-nares." Her words were cynical and Slade hated her for it. "They pull millionaires." She continued. "Not everybody gets invited and not everybody knows about them either.

But I do." She pointed to herself. "They play in a mobile trailer because they can control the address and players. Don't like a location? They just drive somewhere else. This shit is very organized, trust me." She moved closer to Slade. "You rob this party and you will get the biggest payout you've ever imagined."

Killa laughed and shook his head. "With all do respect, you don't know the money we touched, little white Lily. A nigga might be on his dick now with no funds but let me check you right quick on your assumptions."

"Exactly," Slade added.

"My apologies." She swallowed. "I did jump out there but that's because I want this to work." She looked at all of them. "But can I count on you or not? The last thing I want to do is waste my own time."

Slade sighed. "Let me talk to my brothers first. Alone."

Lily stood up. "Okay, but it has to be tonight. If we don't hit them then the next game won't be until five months from now." She walked out of the room.

Slade and his brothers stood up and faced one another. "So what we gonna do?" Audio asked excitedly rubbing his hands together. "I told you this broad was gonna give us a payout. See what I'm saying now? Ain't you glad I convinced you to roll with her, Slade? You would've had us out a lot of paper."

Slade glared at Audio. "Shut the fuck up, lil nigga." He pointed at him. "I'm still mad at how you been moving lately."

He frowned. "Me?" He pointed to himself. "What I do 'cept save the day?"

"You acting like you never fucked a white broad in your life," Killa added.

"Hold up, is that what ya'll think this is about?"

Slade and Killa stared at him.

"Well it ain't about that."

"Then what is it about? Enlighten us." Killa questioned. "'Cause we ain't come out here for no pink slit. We all agreed on a plan and we want to stick to it for our brother."

Audio frowned. "So Slade gets to get some On The Run Pussy and I don't?"

Slade ran his hand down his face again. He was killing his mood with his immaturity. "You know what, me and Killa gonna make the move." Slade walked to the bed. "And you gonna stay here." Killa grabbed one of the ripped bed sheets and Slade grabbed another.

Audio frowned, his hands extended in front of him. "Hold up, what's that for anyway, man?" He looked at Slade.

Slade tied the first sheet around his mouth while Killa used the other for his hands. When they were done Audio was mummy wrapped and connected to the bed, with nothing but his nostrils out for breath.

Loving their work, Slade and Killa winked and walked out. Laughing all the way.

CHAPTER FIFTEEN

FARAH

"Don't refuse to do something because you've
never done it. It's a waste of living."

A red ceramic bowl with vanilla cake batter sat on
the counter as Farah whipped slowly. Although
it seemed she was being meticulous about the mixture
being smooth, in actuality she was thinking about her
life and Cutie was watching, trying desperately to read
her mind.

"I'm glad they let you out today." She looked at
Farah's bruised face. "They locked me in that room
while you were gone. I wanted to see you so badly."

Silence.

"Did they hurt you?" Cutie asked. "When you
were in there?"

Farah smiled, not wanting to talk about being
raped, or what they put her through. Truth was she
knew why they were getting worse. They weren't
being taken care of. "Did you grease the pans?"

"The pans?"

"The cake pans I asked you to grease when I told
you we were baking."

"Oh…uh yes." She slid off the barstool and walked toward the blood colored Aga stove, grabbed the pans and moved them back to Farah. "Here they are." She paused. "But, I don't know why we baking. Shouldn't we be trying to get out of this house?"

"Nobody leaves unless Bones wants us too. Haven't you got that point by now?" Farah stared out into the kitchen, thoughts of Gregory and Swanson running through her mind. "Now are they greased?"

"Yes," she pouted.

"Good," she stopped mixing. "Now come here." Cutie stood in front of her and Farah stood behind her. "Pour the batter slowly."

Cutie looked back at her. "But I've never done this before."

"Don't refuse to do something because you've never done it. It's a waste of living." Cutie nodded and under Farah's watchful eyes she slowly poured the batter into the first and then the second pan. "You see…if you take your time…all things work out in the end." Farah observed as the mixture lay smoothly before her.

"Farah, your sister is here. Bones has approved your visit." Eve, one of the members of The Fold said.

Farah nodded. "I'm coming now."

THE FOLD

"Look at your face, Farah," Mia sighed. "And this is what you wanted? All to drink blood?"

"You know that's not the case." She rubbed her own arms like she was on drugs. "Well blood is only one part of it but that's not the only reason I'm staying."

"Then what do you want me to say?" Mia whispered as she stood next to Farah's bed. "That I warned you these people were trouble? That I never wanted you involved with them in the first place? If so you've heard it all before."

"No but this is different." Her breath increased. "He…he's trying to break me."

"This is what you told me and Shadow you could handle. So what now? You telling me that you can't? If that's the case why not just leave?"

Farah walked away and stood next to the door. "I can't go because if I do…you know what'll happen to you and Shadow."

Mia moved slowly toward her. "First off Shadow is deep in the streets these days. With grandma dead and pops locked up, can't nothing stop him from fucking all these bitches and selling dope." She exhaled. "So I'd be surprised if anybody would be able to find him, let alone Bones. And me, you know I'm good. Besides all that I'm ready to die for you. All you have to do is say the word." She paused and moved closer to Farah. "Still got that phone I sneaked into you?"

Farah nodded yes.

"When you need me. When you're ready to leave. Use it. It's as simple as that."

Farah looked downward. "Ain't no use. I'm trapped. Forever."

Mia grew annoyed because Farah was blowing her. She knew Bones had done a good job of breaking her spirit. "Do you remember when you first moved out the house? When you got that apartment and them fucked up roommates?"

Farah smiled. "How can I forget?"

"I was angry at first but what I saw in you was your strength. You been through a lot and that gives you experience, Farah. Use who you are to get what you want. Whatever that may be." She placed her hand on Farah's cheek. "Don't let him beat you down to

THE FOLD

make himself feel better." She moved her hand and pointed at her. "Unless it's part of your plan. Think. Hard. You smarter than him. He just doesn't know it."

Farah stood naked in front of the mirror. Age had made her body more curvaceous and her eyes more seductive. She couldn't believe she allowed people and circumstances to make her forget who she really was.

A woman.

A killer

A seductress.

A Vamp.

Never again would she play co-star in anybody else's production, especially not Bones. Starting from that moment, she would turn the situation around to work for her and there would be nothing anyone could do to stop her.

It was time for a bloody war.

"Bones. Here I come."

ZASHAY

Zashay rushed down the steps and up to the fireplace in the living room area of the basement. Looking behind herself every so often, to make sure no one was coming, she flipped the switch for the automatic fireplace and it turned on, glowing lightly. Afterwards she removed the book Mooney wrote from under her shirt and tossed it into the fire. She swiped it during their love making session and she was pleased with herself when Bones was so focused on fucking her that he didn't even know it was missing.

That was all she needed.

A little time to sneak it away.

When the pages crackled she felt some relief because the last thing she needed was Bones finding out anymore nonsense about her from its pages, especially after proposing. Nothing was going to stop her from being with him. From being his queen, including Mooney snitching from the grave. As she saw the journal light up in flames she realized she was definitely glad to be done with the book and it's secrets.

Once and for all.

For a brief second she thought about the beginning.

CHAPTER SIXTEEN

THE FOLD

THE PAST

"Trust me and I promise I will make it worth your wild."

*T*hey were all sitting on the floor of a vacant home that was up for sale. It belonged to Dr. Weil and was just one of the many properties he owned around the world. He had given them all cups of tea and blankets to warm them up but the thirteen were still concerned about what was to happen next.

"So uh, I'm still confused," Lewis said. "I mean why bring us here?" He looked around from where he sat.

"Yeah, is this your spot?" Porter asked.

"Yes...well...it's one of them." He paused. "I have so many that they're hard to keep up with." He smiled. "So I'm selling this one to clear up a little of my business."

"Now the nigga bragging," Porter said shaking his head.

"So what now?" Lewis continued. "We just hang in here and stare at each other like we crazy?"

"Let me make things crystal. If we go back to Crescent, you will be killed and I will be arrested for taking you off the property. I can't have that." He scratched his head. "I need people to think when they see me out that I have no connection with you. And I need them to think you all have died."

They moved uncomfortably where they sat.

"So what does that mean?" Giovanna asked.

"I have some land in rural Maryland. It's very isolated and there's a house there too. It hasn't been lived in for a while so it will need fixing up. A lot. But if you help me, I'll provide you with a safe haven and food."

Porter jumped up. "I knew he was a faggy," he paused. "He want us to move in so he can fuck us all whenever he get ready. I'm out of here."

"All or none," Dr. Weil said in a low voice.

Porter turned toward him but stayed near the door.

"What you say?" Lewis asked.

"I said all of you have to agree," Dr. Weil clarified, nodding at Porter. "If he leaves I won't help any of you. Because like I said they need to believe that every one of you died in that fire. So, we have to decide right now if the thirteen of you are going to trust me or not. The good thing is, that even though I didn't get your medicine from the facility I can still help you."

"Wait, we have to go un-medicated too?" Courtney asked with raised brows. "Because, I'm not allowed to be without it for — "

"I haven't been totally honest." Dr. Weil swallowed. "There's another reason I wanted you all to come with me. I have created a medical plan that I believe will cure your illnesses in the short term but if repeated it will work for a lifetime. That is, if you trust me and give up the lives you all knew and can stand a little pain. Trust me and I promise I will make it worth your wild."

"So you want us to be guinea pigs?"

"My plan will work! It's a new approach to medicine that the medical industry wasn't ready for. I'm before my time but I always have been. Give me a chance and through me you will be able to live out your dreams." He paused. "I'll leave you to talk about it alone." He disappeared into the house.

Lewis stood up. "What we gonna do?" He looked at everyone.

Porter moved closer. "I don't know about y'all but I'm bouncing."

"And then what, man? Die in the cold? Maybe get up with some of your old friends who already got word that you crazy?" Lewis asked.

"He's right you know?" Laverne said. "As wild as Dr. Weil looks, right now he's daddy."

"I don't know about all that but I'm willing to see what he's planning," Morton, who had been mostly quiet said. "Ride this out with us, Porter. Right now, we all the family you got. Like it or not."

"Before you say anything I heard the good doctor has a fetish," Laverne said to everyone. "For pain." She shrugged. "Ain't got a lot more info other than that. But you can bet whatever plan he has for us involves it."

"And that should make us scared?" Morton asked. "After everything we've been through at Crescent?"

"Different things scare different men. I'm just giving you facts."

Dr. Weil walked back into the room and looked at all of them. Each one of them rose to their feet and nodded.

"We're with you," Morton said. "But I think we should change our names. Part with the old ones to leave the past behind."

Dr. Weil smiled. "You don't say much but when you do you speak volumes." He clapped his hands together. "So let me hear what you're gonna call yourselves."

Laverne raised her hand. "Call me Mooney. I've always liked that name."

"Call me Mayoni," Giovanna said. "No particular reason."

Dr. Weil looked around. "Okay…anyone else?"

"Call me Jasmine," Courtney said.

"Nah…I hate that name," Porter interjected. "Used to fuck with a bitch with the same name and I wanted her dead every day of her life." He paused. "But you can call me Gregory though."

"Okayyyy," she said a little freaked out. "Call me Zashay then." She shrugged.

Dr. Weil nodded.

"Call me Carlton," Lewis said.

One by one they went around the room giving their monikers, which the doctor with his good memory memorized instantly. "So we have Mayoni, Carlton, Zashay, Nicola, Denny, Phoenix, Wesley, Gregory, Swanson, Vivica, Eve and Lootz." He looked at Morton. "Hold up, you didn't tell me what your name is yet."

"Oh…I can't think of a good one. So for now just call me Bones."

CHAPTER SEVENTEEN

SLADE

"The nigga ain't coming so it's a done deal."

"I still don't think we have enough people," Lily said pacing the floor of her motel room. "I mean, why did you tell Audio to stay behind because it's not smart? This type of job needs as many hands as possible." Her skin was reddening and he could tell she was scared.

Slade wiped his hand down his face. "Look, if this 'bout money who cares who's with us?" Slade asked. "Me and my brother ready and we got this. So take us and stop worrying about Audio. The nigga ain't coming so it's a done deal."

"Exactly," Killa added. "We did this type shit before. We know what we doing."

She blew a raspberry. "I hear all that but there will be a lot of people who may be armed there tonight. Trust me, if I thought both of you would be enough I wouldn't say anything." She paused. "I'm sorry but I don't think you'll be able to handle it. Maybe some other time."

"There you go again trying to make assumptions on what our lives have been about." Slade glared. "When I tell you me and my brother got it that's the fuck what I mean." He paused. "What we really should be asking is who got you so fucked up that you would pull something like this? Because I know you know these dudes."

She sighed and flopped on the edge of the bed. "My business is my business just like yours is yours." She fell backwards on the thin mattress. "And I'm sorry about me keep pressing the issue about Audio. Guess I just wanted him there that's all."

Slade looked at Killa.

Once again his instincts told him that she was scandalous but the need for money blinded him at the moment. Sure he could've had Killa take eyes off Memory and his son whom was named Deal Baker to bring them some money since they didn't have an ID for Western Union. But he was afraid that if Memory had an opportunity, she'd hurt the kid again.

Then there was the clan of Bakers, who would've dropped everything to be involved in a score with their cousins if Slade made a call. The problem with extended family was they talked too much and he was certain that with time and the way they ran their mouths, The Fold would know their plans to get at Farah before they reached their destination.

"Tell me again who these people are," Slade asked her.

She sighed. "Well Quion is the main one. He sets up the games and the people who he trusts sends out word on the location. So it starts around noon but I've seen them play up to midnight sometimes if the pot is right."

"How many people do you think be there?" Killa questioned. "I mean, how do we know it'll be worth it?"

"I can't tell you how many people because the players change. But I will say they start with a minimum bid of twenty thousand, enough income to make it worthwhile." She looked at both of them. "So you tell me if it's worth your time."

Slade nodded. "If I find out this a set up I'll kill you." He pointed at her. "With my bare hands. Just so you know."

She frowned. "Wait a minute. I'm the one who brought you in on this. How you gonna — "

"Do you hear me?" Slade continued moving closer. "If I get an idea that anything is wrong I'ma knock your chin off your shoulders. Just letting you know where I'm coming from."

She folded her arms across her chest tightly and poked out her lips. "So much for hospitality." She stormed to the bathroom and slammed the door.

Killa walked up to his brother. "What you thinking, Slade?"

"That we got a fifty/fifty chance of dying."

Killa nodded. "For some reason it's a chance I'm willing to take."

"Guess we going then." Slade looked at him and they both broke out into laughter.

CHAPTER EIGHTEEN

FARAH

"We are about Blood, Sex and Pain."

Farah was seated on the edge of the bed looking outward when the door opened and Nicola walked inside. "You okay? Because you been moping around the house all day." She asked. "And I was so worried about you and being with Gregory alone."

"I'm fine." Farah paused. "Just thinking about a few things."

"I wanted to ask you for a courtesy."

Farah didn't have time for many favors but Nicola had always been good to her so she humored her for the moment. "What is it?"

"Carlton...he..."

Farah sighed. "You still crushing on him?"

"Kinda." She sat next to her.

"Carlton loves Mayoni. You know he'll never—"

"I know, I know." She looked down. "I just..." Nicola shook her head, unable to say much more. Turning toward her she said, "I wanted him first you know? On the day Dr. Weil rescued us from Crescent. But Mayoni always had a thing for whoever was in charge at the time and powerful men love her back. During that time, when we first got here, me and Carlton spent a lot of time together. Made love a few times and everything. But then Mayoni saw how close he was with Dr. Weil and how much he was letting him do for our family and he left me for her. She assured him that she could make him next in charge, except it was Bones instead. I don't think Dr. Weil ever liked her." She exhaled. "Always the brides panties never the dress."

Farah frowned. "Don't think that's how the saying goes."

"But that's how I feel."

Farah nodded.

"So me and Lootz got together but he never really did it for me." Nicola shook her head. "And now look, Porter's dead and —"

Nicola, I don't mean to be rude but —"

"Have you drank recently?" She paused. "I'm talking about blood? Your face is really bruised and flushed. You need to refresh."

"No."

Nicola stood up and walked in front of Farah and pushed her back on the bed. Next she crawled on top of her easing a blade from the pocket on her bra.

THE FOLD

Looking down at Farah she said, "Damn you're sexy. You wanna do the honors?" She extended the razor.

Farah removed the gold blade from her fingertips and sliced into Nicola's shoulder. When the blood appeared she sucked it lightly, savoring the salty flavor oozing on her tongue. And after a few more slits Farah's mind was right and she was ready for the world.

Farah smoothed out the silky black dress she was wearing and stood in the mirror to look at herself. Although sometimes she preferred to dress down, she did appreciate that The Fold's motto was glamour over everything. Besides, it felt good to have the smooth Versace designer dress against her skin and in all truth she was killing it. Cutie stood next to her and admired Farah's reflection through the mirror. "You look different today." She paused. "Why?"

Farah looked over at her. "I am different."

Cutie smiled. "I wanna be just like you."

"What does that mean?"

"A vamp!"

Farah giggled. "I'm more than just that, Cutie. And I keep trying to stress that in this house everything is not what it seems." She took a deep breath. "Besides, there was a long road for me to become who I am, and I'm still not done." She ran her hands down her hips. "Not even close."

Cutie looked at the door as she had several times that day.

"Who you waiting on?"

Cutie grinned. "Phoenix."

Farah nodded. "Fuck him yet?"

"Ewww! Gross!"

"I know you've had sex, Cutie so cut the games. And the other men can smell it on you. I won't tell you how I feel about Phoenix because D.C. knows how I used to get down back in the day. But still...be careful with him."

Cutie frowned. "Why you say that?"

Cutie walked away and Farah looked at her from the mirror. "This house was created to satisfy the flesh. Don't get me wrong, I love most of the people here but I'm never under any illusions that it's anything different. We are about Blood, Sex and Pain. "

"I don't understand."

"That's why you don't belong here."

The door opened and the youngest member of The Fold, Phoenix walked inside without knocking, something that burned Farah up about him every time. Outside of his good looks he also brought with him a scent of cologne and Farah already knew he was about to lay the pipe on her hard. "Hi, Farah." He waved and then looked at Cutie. "You ready?"

She smiled and walked toward him, looking back at Farah once before following him out, closing the door behind herself.

Farah wasn't dumb.

She knew Phoenix was a plant to keep Cutie happy in the house by Bones, since for whatever reason Farah had grown to care for the girl. The more reasons he had for her to stay the better. But Farah could not be distracted. Besides, after speaking with her sister she'd come up with a plan to escape The Fold and go on with her life and she was putting it into action. Although it would take some work she was up to the challenge.

Zashay stood at the foot of the bed while staring at Bones whose dick was at a partial thickness as he looked at her curvaceous body. He was stroking briskly to get it at full attention.

She looked over at him and grinned. "Ready for me yet?"

"Give me a second," he said biting his bottom lip. "I just want to stare at you for a moment."

She smiled and ran her hand down the curves of her body. "Soon you're going to be calling me Mrs. Bones." She grinned harder thinking about the day. "And I'm gonna love it too."

He chuckled. "Is that right?"

"Dead ass. Do you realize how long it took me to get to this moment? To this day? Since we've come here the only thing I wanted was you." He tried to keep a straight face even though she reminded him incessantly about her obsession over him and in all honestly it was getting boring. "And now — "

The door opened slowly and Farah strutted inside. She picked up Zashay's robe and stuffed it in her hands. "Get out, Zashay. The games are over."

Zashay frowned. "Fuck you doing in here?"

"You really want me to say it again?" Farah said calmly. "Bounce!"

THE FOLD

"What...you..." Zashay looked at Bones for help. "Can you tell her to leave before I have to scratch her face off?"

As Zashay rambled Farah noticed that Bones' dick was now rock hard. "Aye, Zashay, let me holla at Farah for a minute. I'll get up with you later."

"Bones!" Zashay cried. "But you promised! You promised you would never do this to—"

"Get the fuck out!" He yelled. "Now!"

Zashay took several breaths, slipped on her robe and tied it tightly. Quickly she walked out, closing the door behind her.

"You know you just set her off right?" Bones asked. "She gonna be mad as fuck about it too."

"And we gonna fake like you really care? She eased toward the bed, crawled on top of it and stood over his body. "And we gonna fake like everything you did wasn't to get my attention? 'Cause I can go get her now if you want her in here instead of me."

"Stop playing and get down here."

Slowly she eased her body down and raised her dress, until his dick was tucked inside of her like a gun in a holster. "Wow, you feel like you miss me."

He grabbed her waist and pumped in and out of her until his body trembled. "I ain't saying shit else to swell up your head. You already know what it is with me and you." He paused. "The question is are you done fighting with me or not?"

"I'm done. How can I fight a man who always wins?"

She placed her palms on his chest and rode him until she could feel him pulsating. "You gonna tell everybody who the real boss is right? And who really stands at your side?" He nodded. "That means Mayoni too?"

"You know I will." His tongue hung out the side of his mouth.

"Let me hear you say it."

"You're the queen." He paused, gripping her waist harder. "I did all of this crazy shit for you, sexy," he moaned. "I just wanted you to notice me. Sorry I had to fuck up your face. You still pretty though."

She smiled as he reveled in the softness of her silky pocket. *Weak ass nigga.* She thought to herself. *And you wonder why I could never fuck with you.*

After showering in her room, Farah placed her black velvet sweat suit on for comfort. When she walked back into the bathroom she was surprised that Swanson was standing there, watching her. "What the fuck?" She yelled, touching her chest. "You almost...killed me!"

"How you doing?"

"What you doing in my bathroom?" She paused. "As a matter of fact! Just get out!" She pointed at the door.

Farah limped out of her room and into the hallway, blood smeared all on her face and chest. Confused, Bones walked up on her just as Swanson came out. "What's going on?" He glared.

"I...he...," Farah ran back into the room, leaving Bones and Swanson alone. He approached Swanson and observed the blood on his hands. "I was just fooling around with her some." He paused. "Sorry, man." He cleared his throat. "I guess she wasn't feeling it."

"Off limits," Bones said.

I know, man. I was just—"

"Don't tell me that you know and then give me an excuse." He shoved him into the wall. "She's mine and what I allowed to happen that day was then. This is now."

"Never again, man."

Bones glared at him once more and walked away.

CHAPTER NINETEEN

SLADE

"You haven't wronged me or my brother. Yet"

Slade, Killa and Lily were crouched behind the trailer where they already knocked out two men who were on guard to protect the game. They were doing a bad job too because they were two soldiers short. Needing to see inside, slowly Slade rose and peered into the window. When he saw what he wanted he lowered. "They playing now."

"How many you see?" Killa asked.

"About five or six," he paused. "But we can take them."

Lily grinned. "Good, I'm gonna go in and try to throw them off our plan." She rose up and dusted off her clothing. "When I scratch my head come inside. I'll pick up whatever I can find and help when the time comes."

Yeah right, dirty bitch. Slade thought.

When Lily disappeared, they both cocked the weapons she gave them earlier. They were .45s with gold handles and they were unique. "You sure this will work?" Killa asked.

"Nah…but we gonna take a chance. Besides," he paused. "Didn't you say you wanted a little adventure?"

"Nah…that was Audio."

Slade laughed. "Well that time has come."

Quion slid several stacks of one hundred dollar bills onto the poker table after making his bid, when the door opened and Lily waltzed inside he smiled at her. "Wow, you finished acting like a brat already?" He scratched through one of the bushy cornrows on his head. "If so this a record. It normally takes a few days for you to come around."

Everyone laughed.

"Guess I got tired of fighting with you." Lily flopped on his lap despite irritating the fuck out of the players due to being too close to the cards. "Just wanted a little attention that's all. Maybe you should give it to me."

"Well now you—"

Suddenly the door flew open and Slade and Killa busted inside, guns in the air. To let folks know they weren't playing they sounded a bullet off into the ceiling and then aimed at the men who were caught off guard. Most everyone was strapped at the game but one false move and Slade would've reacted quicker than they could've grabbed their weapons.

Lily on the other hand wanted to shit on her thong because she hadn't expected the country boys to be aggressive so soon. Not only had Slade's presence seemed bigger than it had when she first pulled up on him, but she had yet to give him the sign to enter.

So what was he doing there?

"I don't know who you are, but you came in on the wrong game." Quion warned. "So I suggest you turn back while you still can."

"I'ma do all that but first I got something you want."

Quion frowned. "And what the fuck is that?"

"Information."

Quion sat back in his seat and Lily rose, easing slowly back into the wall. This didn't look good for her.

"You got the floor." He raised his hands and they dropped at his sides. "So let me hear it." He crossed his arms over his chest.

"Now I could've come in here and robbed the game as planned," he looked around the room. "But I'm not gonna do that."

"And why not?" He gritted his teeth.

"Because you haven't wronged me or my brother." He paused and gave him a serious stare. "Yet."

"Make your point quicker," Player #2 added.

Slade frowned at him. "I come in peace," Slade warned Player #2. "Don't make me change my mind and take a few niggas with me to the afterlife."

"Shut the fuck up, man!" Quion said to Player #2 pointing at him. He focused back on Slade. "Continue. 'Cause I have to know what inspired you to interrupt my game."

Slade glared. "Lily sent us."

Quion looked at him sideways. "Who that?"

Slade frowned and looked at the only bitch in the room, who stood so close to the wall she looked like a picture. "Her." He pointed. "Ain't that her name?"

"You mean my wife?" His nostrils flared.

Slade laughed. He knew she was scandalous. "I don't know about who she is but I'm telling you that,

that broad sent us to rob this game. Now I don't know why but that's what we're here for. To take all ya'll's shit."

"Do me a favor and kill these niggas!" Quion said, as Player #2, #3 and #4 aimed at them.

"Look at these fucking guns!" Slade yelled, standing in front of Killa who tried to get back on his side. Slade would give his life for his brother but Killa didn't want to be protected; he wanted to fight arm and arm. "Look at our fucking guns!"

Quion raised his hand to stop his men from making the scene bloodier than need be. Slowly he rose, walked toward Slade and took the weapon from his hand. The mere fact that Slade let him at the gun, basically unarming himself, already gave Quion enough reason to trust him.

A little.

After further inspection Quion frowned. "This...this my hammer." He turned around and looked at his wife. "April, what is this shit?"

So that's her name. Slade thought.

"He's lying, babe," Lily peeled herself off the wall. "I would never—"

"But you did though," Quion said cutting her off. "You did do this shit didn't you? Gave them my guns and everything."

"But...but I..." Pee rolled down her leg and dampened her pink espadrilles.

"All this because I didn't want you at the pool party Saturday?" He paused. "And you thought I was fucking that bitch?" He yelled. "For some light shit you would do this to me? Possibly getting me killed?"

"Correction, I walked in on you fucking her, Quion!" She yelled, face blood red with rage. "But you didn't see me or know I was there! You had her in our pool house, banging her from behind! With my family in the same house! What about our son?"

Quion, embarrassed beyond reason, wiped his hand down his face and took a deep breath. He walked over to the table, grabbed several stacks of cash equaling twenty thousand. He handed that money to Slade. "Take this...I'm buying my life back."

Slade looked down at the money in his hand. "Thanks, man."

"No problem. Not too often you find real niggas out here." He gave him back the gun too. "So by law you gotta reward the shit when you see it. Ain't enough of us no more. Ya'll can keep the hammers."

"Can I ask you for one more favor?" Slade said.

"I'm listening." Quion crossed his arms over his chest.

"That's your red Impala outside?"

Quion grinned.

Slade and Killa strolled toward the Impala and unlocked the car door. Twenty stacks heavier. "Wow, we really made it out of this shit alive." Killa paused. "But why you ain't let me in on the plan though?"

Slade smiled. "I changed it at the last minute."

Killa nodded. "How you know he would give over the keys to his car?"

"We saved the nigga's life. You heard him. 'Cause of us, he got rid of that scandalous bitch." Slade eased inside. "Giving us the car is probably light weight shit to him anyway. You saw all that money in the room. Trust me."

Suddenly their was a female scream followed by gunfire and Killa looked at Slade before rushing into the car. "But let's get out of here before his good graces go bad."

Slade nodded. "You ain't never lied. It's off to D.C."

CHAPTER TWENTY

MAYONI

"You're a nosey fucker, you know that right?"

Mayoni walked into the bathroom where Cutie was on the floor scrubbing tiles with bleach, something she assigned her to do earlier for the party that was going on later. The bathroom was next to the pool area and she wanted it spotless. Plus it did her heart good to see Farah's lackey get her hands dirty for a change. "Almost done? You been in here all day." Mayoni asked crossing her arms over her chest.

Cutie looked at Mayoni and rolled her eyes.

Mayoni giggled. "No need in you being mad at me. Everybody in this house works in one-way or another. Why should your red ass get a free ride?"

Mayoni was about to leave when Cutie asked, "What happened to Mooney's arm? And give me the truth."

Mayoni turned around and glared. "You grown ain't you? What I tell you 'bout asking questions?"

"Did Farah cut it off?" She paused. "Or was it Bones?"

"You're a nosey fucker, you know that right?"

"I gotta find out. I mean nobody talks to me around here. Everybody treats me like a kid. Even Farah."

Mayoni leaned against the wall and observed Cutie. Something about the little girl she liked and it irritated her. Still, it felt good that Cutie came to her with a question she wanted to know instead of Farah. She exhaled deeply. "They both were responsible."

"How?" Cutie sat the sponge down.

"Farah found out that Mooney was writing a book about our lives at Crescent and what we had going on here."

"Crescent?" She was confused.

"Look, did you even read the book Mooney wrote?" She paused. "You know what, I'm done with story time, Farah gotta tell you the rest." She threw her hands up in the air.

"Oh yeah, the crazy house. I remember reading that part now. Please finish."

Mayoni frowned. "You trying to get slapped?"

"What I do now?" She shrugged.

"Calling it a crazy house disrespects my team." She sighed. "Anyway Farah mentioned to Bones that Mooney was writing a book. But before he could approach her he caught Mooney going into his room trying to steal notes that Dr. Weil gave him. She'd

188   ***THE FOLD***

already been thrown out at that time. Mad at the world he cut off her arm for stealing and Farah felt guilty about it so she helped her escape the Ice Box he threw Mooney in."

"Wow."

"I give you all that, and the only thing you can say is wow?" She paused. "Look, girl, just finish cleaning. We got celebrating to do. Shikar is back on?"

"Shikar?"

"The hunt!" Mayoni threw her hands up in annoyance. "I'm done with you! Finish cleaning." Mayoni stormed out."

ZASHAY

Zashay hustled down the hallway eager for dinner. Earlier Nicola and Eve had told her the chef was serving lobster with crab rice and she was hungry as fuck just thinking about it. She was almost in the dining room when Gregory stepped in front of her. "Hey, sexy, where you going?" He gripped his dick, something he'd done a lot lately.

"To eat." She backed up a little. "Why?"

"Did you wanna play around some first?' He removed his razor. "I cut and lick and then you do the same?" His eyes were glassed over and she knew the experience would not be enjoyable in the least. Out of all of them, he and Swanson needed their medication the most.

"But I'm—" He yanked her by the arm; squeezing her wrist so hard her fingertips went numb.

"Play with me. I just want a little taste. Dinner gonna be there."

"Okay…okay, Gregory. But you're hurting me."

"Then stop playing hard to get." He released.

"Where are we going?"

"Your room is closer." He grinned. "So move."

Slowly she turned around and he followed. She trembled as she walked toward her room, doing her best not to show fear. Playing with Gregory lately had never been enjoyable but what could she do? She couldn't shake him if she tried, especially since Bones knocked her down from grace.

When they made it to her room she closed the door and he whipped out his dick as if it were a gun. Sweat covered his forehead and his tongue hung out as if he hadn't a thing to drink all day. "Get on the floor."

"Gregory, I don't want to have sex. Can't we just drink?" She smiled.

"Why? You ain't trying to fuck me or something? My dick ain't no good." He paused. "Bones is done with you. You might as well have some fun."

"It's just that last time you hurt me really bad."

"Fuck all of that! Get on the floor." He pointed in the corner.

The moment she sat down he stuffed his dick into her mouth roughly. And although her teeth scraped at the sides of his dick, he didn't seem to care. When she looked down at his penis she saw many old scratches and believed he was used to women pawing at it to get away.

When he felt himself about to cum, he gripped her throat and squeezed tightly, cutting off all air circulation. The harder he squeezed the weaker she became until she passed out. And when she did, he continued to jerk off until he came into her mouth.

Eve was in the backyard setting fire to rats, something she did in her free time and what also led into her being in Crescent. Over the past few days she collected a few garden rats for the purpose of torture and like she had in the past, she just poured gasoline on one and set it on fire when suddenly it leapt up and ran. Afraid it would run into the house she gave chase.

The last thing she needed was it getting inside and setting something on fire, revoking her membership in The Fold. Although Dr. Weil was the one who said her habit had to stop or she'd be banned, she was certain that Bones would still uphold the law, especially if she burned everything down.

When she cornered the rat up against the wall, she stomped it hard and bent down to pick it up. The moment she did she peered into the window to see who had seen her and was shocked when she saw Zashay lying on the floor as if she were dead.

"What the fuck?"

Eve wiped cum and blood off Zashay's face. When her eyes opened she breathed a sigh of relief. "Oh my God, Zashay. What happened?"

Zashay sat up slowly and pulled her legs toward her. "It was Gregory." She felt so weak.

Eve frowned. "We have to do something about him." She paused. "Maybe we should tell Bones."

"No, he doesn't care about me anymore. Or what the men do."

"Then who should we go to?"

"Next in power. Farah."

The weather was perfect and because of it The Fold decided to have an impromptu barbeque, in celebration of Shikar. The pool was crowded with the members partially dressed, drunk and loud and it was the best mood everyone had been in, in a long time.

Bones stood up against the inside of the pool while Farah was in front of him, her legs wrapped around his body as they waded in the warm water. Her red and gold bikini made her stand out from everyone wearing black swimsuits and it was just the way he loved it. "Damn you fine," he said.

"Nobody can ever tell me you not feeling me." She kissed his neck and one of the dreads fell free from the bun he was wearing on top of his head.

"When you want someone you gotta let them know." He paused. "But are you really ready to be with me?" He asked looking into her eyes.

She smiled and touched the side of his face. "You think too deeply, Bones. Not everything need be so heavy."

He nodded. "Then why do I feel like you have something planned?"

She shrugged. "Well, actually I did want to talk to you about something. There have been a lot of fights and weird situations breaking out in the house and I wanted to know, if I was able to get medication for the people who need it would you let me? That way — "

He grabbed her cheek and squeezed so hard her lips puckered. "Leave it alone. We don't need no more fucking medicine." He released her. "Drop it, Farah." He slapped her ass. "Now go get me a drink."

"No problem." She eased off of him, removed her bikini top and tossed it in the water. Next she walked up the steps slowly leading outside of the pool, capturing Bones' attention, and every man who wanted a taste of the forbidden vamp.

Once at the bar Zashay, who been watching them together, stomped toward her with a major attitude. "That's mighty tasteless of you." She nodded at Farah's breasts.

"No it ain't." Farah winked. "The man likes what he likes. A show. So I'm giving it to him. If you tried it sometimes he might not have dumped you." She focused on the bartender. "A bloody Henny with ice please."

"You know he's playing you right?" Zashay asked. Farah smiled at her as if she was totally irrelevant before focusing back on the bartender. "He wants to tear us apart."

Farah thought the woman was goofy, especially since she'd recently said the same things to her and got knocked down.

"I'll take a bloody martini too," Farah said to the bartender, irritating Zashay beyond know end due to not responding.

Zashay grabbed her arm. "Can you talk to me? Please? I want to talk to you about something."

Farah turned toward her and looked into her eyes. For a moment Zashay's stare fell on her breasts before rolling up. Her body was perfect and that only added to Zashay's fury. "What?"

"I'm sorry for—"

"You fucked up with me," Farah said. I don't want to hear much else.

"Excuse me?"

"I haven't trusted a woman since my sister and I trusted you." She pointed at her. "But what did you do, choose a man who treated you like shit over us. And now look...the nigga dumped you the moment I gave the word." She paused. "And to think, I don't even want him."

Zashay frowned. "What does that mean?"

"Just what I said."

"So you have plans to do something I don't know about?"

"Even if I did, why would I tell you?"

Silence.

Zashay took a deep breath. "Look, we have to live together and—"

"We don't have to do anything but stay out of each other's way. And when the time comes, you will do everything in your power to convince me why I shouldn't kill you for choosing the wrong side." Farah picked up the drinks on the bar. "Oh, and don't bother telling Bones about any of this. I'll just lie my face off and cry. And trust me, he *will* believe me. He always does." She walked away.

Breasts bouncing all the way.

Mad at the world, Mayoni sat on the lawn chair next to Carlton as she glared at Farah and Zashay from a far. "What do you think they were talking about? They looked awfully heated don't you think?"

He looked over at them. "Who cares?"

"I care!" Slowly her head rotated toward him. "Why aren't you ambitious?" She threw her hands up. "I mean really."

He frowned.

"I'm serious, Carlton! Answer me! Why don't you try to figure out how to make yourself indispensible to Bones? The way you moving now there's no reason for you to stay around or be in his circle. In case you forgot Bones is it for The Fold and Dr. Weil is gone."

He nodded his head. "You know what, you're right. There is absolutely no reason for me to stay around. Goodbye, bitch." He got up and walked over to Nicola.

The moment he walked toward her and tapped her on the shoulder Nicola lit up when she stared into his handsome face. He helped her to her feet and they held a great conversation.

Mayoni felt gut punched as she watched him laugh with her so easily. Sure it was nothing for members to share in one another, but he was making her believe that they could be together if she acted right.

"You wanna play games, Carlton?" Mayoni said to herself. "Okay. We'll play games." With that she leaned back in her chair and sipped her blood red margarita as she thought of the best way to get revenge.

CUTIE

Cutie sat on Phoenix' lap as he played dominoes with three other members of The Fold by the pool. There wasn't a moment that didn't go by that she didn't think about leaving the mansion, but she was falling for Phoenix and he had her wanting to risk it all.

"Domino, bitch ass nigga!" Phoenix yelled as he slammed it down on the table.

"Fuck!" A few of the other members yelled.

"I think you be cheating, son." One of them said, pointing his way.

"He be killing ya'll for real." Cutie laughed. "But I think he might be cheating too." She kissed his cheek. "I mean how many times did you win, bae? Four?"

Phoenix looked at her sideways. "You serious? You believing what these niggas saying out here?"

"I mean I don't know," she said playfully. "It do seem suspect to me though."

He looked at the members and shook his head. "Get up, Cutie."

She rose slowly, noticing how his attitude changed instantly. "Wait...you mad at me? 'Cause I was just playing."

He stood up and stormed away from the table. She was about to follow him when one of the members said, "Don't do it, Cutie. Just leave him be."

But her youth and ambitious ways didn't allow her to listen and so she followed him into the house anyway, begging him to talk to her the entire way. The moment they were in the confines of the mansion and the brightness from outdoors was replaced with the shade from inside, she was met with a blow to the mouth with a closed fist. Horrified she tried to run outside but he grabbed her by the hair and dragged her to his room. When the doors were locked he hit her again in the nose before striking her in the mouth.

"Please don't hit me again," she cried, extending her arms in front of her. She couldn't believe he snapped so easily. "I'm begging you."

Cold and heartless, he lowered his body and picked her up. Now he looked as if he regretted ever laying hands on her. As if he had two personalities. "I'm sorry...I'm sorry, baby. I'll never hit you again I promise." When she hugged him, he punched her again in the stomach, causing her to drop to the floor. Again he helped her to her feet before apologizing once more. "My bad, Cutie. I don't know...I don't know what's gotten into me. It's just that I care about you so much and I can't stand it when you don't take my side in front of people." He paused and lifted her chin with his finger. "Do you love me?"

Her body trembled with fear. Tears rolled down her cheeks and snot oozed from her nose. "Yes...I...I think so." She responded, not knowing the first thing about love.

"Then you gotta learn never to disrespect me again. Because if you do, I can do much worse." He paused. "You my girl now. And that means I can do with you as I please and there's nothing you can do to change it." He looked at her face. "Look at what you made me do? See, I can't have anybody seeing you like this. So how 'bout you just stay in my room until this heals." He walked toward the door.

"But...where... you going?" she asked barely above a whisper, afraid to irritate him even more.

"The party." He winked. "Ain't you heard? We got stuff to celebrate 'round here. Don't worry though, I'll bring you a piece of cake or something. You'll be fine." He walked out.

CHAPTER TWENTY-ONE

SLADE

"I pulled off the road two times fucking with you,
Audio. I'm not doing it again…"

Slade and Killa walked into the motel room with a box of chicken, fries, soda and a pocket full of money. They smiled when they saw Audio sitting on the edge of the bed, rubbing his temples, the sheets that were wrapped around him to hold him hostage sitting on the floor.

"I see you got out," Slade said jokingly smooching his head with his palm. "How long did it take you?" Slade chuckled loudly.

"Long enough to be mad as fuck."

Killa laughed, pawning Audio's head. "You good though right?"

Audio looked at them, stood up and snatched the chicken bag out Slade's hand. "Fuck ya'll, niggas."

All three of them laughed for a minute. "I hated to do it to you, Audio," Slade said seriously. "But we wanted you safe and safe meant away from that chick. She was trouble in case you didn't know."

Audio nodded. "Man, I was mad at first but now it don't even matter no more. As long as ya'll back." He dug into the bag and grabbed a piece of fried chicken. "So I take it things worked out okay." He bit a big piece.

"Yeah...and we back on the road," Slade said showing him the set of car keys.

"Wait, ya'll took the nigga's ride too?" Audio frowned. "What if he reports it missing?"

"He gave it to us," Killa bragged, taking a wing out the bag. "We ain't have to take shit."

Audio frowned. "Hold up...how that work?" He asked with a mouth full of meat.

"Like I been preaching that bitch was trouble," Slade said pointing at him. "And that's all you need to know."

Audio nodded. "I figured anyway." He sounded sad.

Slade looked at Killa and walked over to Audio. "Look, you been fucking two bitches a day for the longest. You can't bring back Chloe by jumping in and out of every pussy with lips."

Audio frowned. "How you figure I'm trying to do that?"

Silence.

Audio stood up. "Look, that white bitch was just cool and I wanted to stab it and give it back that's all." He shrugged. "Ain't nothing wrong with that so stop tripping."

Killa touched Audio on the shoulder. "You ready to roll? We gotta hit the road again. It ain't safe here."

"Yeah…"

"Good. Now go wash yo ass." Killa frowned. "You smell like you shitted in your drawers."

"When I thought ya'll left me in this bitch I did." Audio nodded.

They fell out laughing.

The Baker Boys were back on the road when Audio saw a black Ford Bronco drive past them. He swore he'd seen the same car earlier. "Aye, I think we being followed." Sitting in the back seat, Audio looked out the window. "As a matter of fact, I'm sure of it."

Slade looked at Killa in the passenger seat and shook his head. "I pulled off the road two times fucking with you, Audio. I'm not doing it again so don't ask." He paused. "If some niggas were following us they would've lit this bitch up by now. We good."

"I'm serious, man!" Audio yelled.

"The only thing you need to be serious about is not smoking whatever shit that bitch gave you earlier." Killa told him. "And what I tell you 'bout pulling on weed you don't know the source of anyway?"

"How you sound? I smoke all the time."

"And you be tripping all the time too!"

Audio took a deep breath and shook his head at his brothers thinking his sightings were a game. All he could do was warn them but being under the influence of weed didn't cause them to take him seriously. So he kept the fact that he saw black hoodies and red script with the letters 'TF' to himself too.

Besides, they acted like they wouldn't care anyway.

CHAPTER TWENTY-TWO

FARAH

"What would make you ever think that that nigga would choose you over me?"

Mayoni walked into Bones' office to speak about pre-hunt only to see Farah at his side. She smiled at them both out of courtesy, although she hated Farah for being there, walked inside and closed the door behind herself. "I hope I'm not interrupting anything." She paused. "Is everything okay?"

"Yes...but I wanted to tell you about a change I'm instituting," Bones said as he flipped a few pages on his desk and sighed. "Effective immediately. You will be in charge of security the night of the party."

"Okay...I guess I can facilitate the hunt and security. It'll be a little much but—"

"No need in you doing both." He paused. "Farah will be in charge of Shikar."

Mayoni's mouth opened and closed. "Wait...why...why? It was my idea remember?"

He nodded. "And it was a good idea too." He paused. "Because of it The Fold will enjoy themselves and we have you to thank for it. But Farah agreed to be my wife and—"

"What a fucking joke!" Mayoni yelled. "How could you put this bitch at your side again when you know she's a snake?"

Bones stood up behind his desk. "What did you just say to me?" He glared.

She scratched her head and then her arms. "I'm sorry but...but I...I don't understand any of this. I have more experience than Farah. She's not even an original Fold member. I brought her here and I've been with you longer and—"

"And I appreciate your help but like I said you are not needed for the hunt." He pointed at his desk. "Do you understand me now?"

Mayoni paced before walking up to the desk. "Bones, please don't do this to me. It's all I have. I had so much planned for that night and if you take me off the project people will start to talk. They'll think I'm not apart of your main team anymore."

He laughed and took a seat behind his desk. "You were always concerned with what other people said. That's part of the reason I want Farah to handle this instead of you. She's much more secure about herself than you ever were."

Tears streamed down Mayoni's face. "Bones, please don't—"

"I'm done!" He waved his hand. "Now leave us alone!"

Slowly Mayoni turned around and walked out. She was halfway down the hallway when Farah approached her from behind. "You know I didn't want it this way right?" She paused. "But you forced my hand."

Mayoni turned around and glared at her. "You don't belong here and yet you act as if you do. I can't wait to see you fall, bitch."

"Instead of starting a fight with me you can't win ask yourself this. What would make you ever think that that nigga would choose you over me? In this life or the next?"

Silence.

Farah's head tilted as she observed her closely. "Oh wait...I keep forgetting, you're in love with him. And because of it you can't think straight. But how is that working out?"

"Fuck you, Farah."

"No...I think I'll pass."

Mayoni smiled and stepped closer. "You wanna play? Well watch what I do next."

THE FOLD

Farah stood up straight. "Whatever you're planning it won't work."

"Are you sure about that?" Mayoni grinned. "Because I say otherwise." She stormed off.

Carlton was in Nicola's room making love to her when Mayoni stormed inside like she owned the place. "Get out, bitch!" She yelled at her. "Now!"

"She doesn't have to go anywhere," Carlton said firmly. "This is her room."

"Maybe she'll want to leave when I tell her about the herpes you got on your dick." She paused. "You may not have a flare up now but I bet you, she doesn't know that you can have one in the future." She looked at Nicola. "Leave whore!"

Nicola's jaw dropped as Carlton quickly ushered her out of the room, only the sheet wrapped around her body. "I'll come get you later." When Nicola was gone he stomped up to her. "You promised you'd never tell anybody that, Mayoni."

"Well I lied."

His nostrils flared. "Why don't you just leave me alone? And shoot your shot with who you really want. Bones."

She rolled her eyes. "Don't be ridiculous you know I don't want him." She exhaled. "So are you two dating now?"

"What do you want, Mayoni?"

She sighed. "I don't want to argue with you." She flopped on the edge of the bed. "I realize that the last few days I haven't been my best and I want to make amends. You're the last person I should be fighting with. My one true friend."

"I don't believe you." He paused. "Now either you tell me the truth or stop wasting my time."

She took a deep breath. "Bones placed Farah in charge of Shikar."

He shook his head, walked over to the edge of the bed and grabbed his robe before placing it on. "Wow. This makes so much fucking sense."

"What you talking about now, Carlton?"

"You didn't come here for me. You came because your precious love interest abandoned you." He paused. "Well I don't want anything to do with it anymore, Mayoni. Or you. I'm not a pillow. You can't cry on me."

"I just don't understand how he could trust her!" Mayoni said going off on a rant, she could care less about how Carlton felt. "After everything I've done for him!"

He looked at her sternly. "Mayoni, what do you want from me now? In this moment? Because I'm busy and all I want to do is get back between Nicola's legs."

Her face turned hot with rage. "The phone. I'm going to give the order."

He frowned. "Hold up, I thought we agreed to only use it if Farah didn't do what she promised with Bones. Sounds like she's at his side now so why order the hit on Slade?"

"Don't worry about all that, I need the phone, Carlton." She stood up and extended her hand, wiggling her fingers. "Give it to me."

"I'm not giving you — "

Suddenly the blade of the pocketknife she was holding entered his belly. The metal crashed against his internal organs, ruining him with every thrust. His eyes flew open as the woman he'd love for many years was taking his life. Tears rolled down her cheek but she was not the least bit worried about what she was doing. She wanted revenge and the hidden phone.

And Carlton's life was a non-factor.

"I know you have it here with you, don't you?" She jabbed him again as his body gave out. "You wouldn't dare leave it in our room. I checked before coming here." She stabbed him again. "Don't worry, I'll find it though."

Carlton dropped on the floor and she hopped over him as if he were trash because in her mind he was. It was time to ransack the room. She pulled up the mattress, looked inside dresser drawers and even a few floorboards. Still, she'd come up empty-handed.

"Where is it?" She said to herself, her breaths heavy with anger. So much sweat poured down over her face her hair clung to her cheeks.

Covered in blood, and partially out of her mind she exited the room and walked down the hall. You see Mayoni, like the other members of The Fold, had a special illness when she was in the institution and without Dr. Weil's help she was certainly going out of control also.

After wrecking her mind on where it could be, finally she reentered the room she shared with Carlton, when times were good. And like Nicola's room, hers was also a mess since she virtually destroyed it looking for the phone earlier.

"Where could you be?" She said to herself.

THE FOLD

Suddenly, as if it glowed, she looked across the room at her jewelry box where she kept the diamonds that Carlton had given her. When she opened the lid, underneath the secret compartment was the phone. Had she thought smaller earlier maybe Carlton would be alive.

Or maybe not.

An insane smile spread across her face when she realized he wasn't Bones so she didn't care.

Picking up the phone she pressed the on button, only to see she had one percent worth of battery life remaining. But it would be all she needed to make the call. Using the speed dial option she pressed number one and was immediately connected.

"Do you still have eyes on Slade?"

"Yep," the person said.

"Good." She exhaled. "Kill him."

CHAPTER TWENTY-THREE

SLADE

"Nothing will stop us. We will be together
eventually."

Killa looked over at Slade as he drove and said, "I
don't think ma hated her as much as you
thought."

Slade grinned and sipped the coke in the holder.
"Yeah right. The last thing she wanted was me being
with Farah Cotton. Especially after Knox died."

"Seriously." Killa bit the hot dog he was holding. "I
really believe she saw something in the girl."

Slade looked at him and focused on the road,
trying to understand if there was any validity to what
he was saying. "You know, ma was the only reason I
didn't go looking for Farah earlier. I felt like...by going
I would be letting her down."

"I feel you. And I remember her looking at her one
time; I'm talking about ma. It was when Farah lived at
that apartment." He laughed. "She said something
about in another time, and under different
circumstances, that she was sure Farah was the right
one for you." He chuckled. "Then she said something

about her attitude being funky but for that moment I could tell she understood what kind of woman she was and why you wanted her."

Slade shook his head. "Never knew that."

Killa nodded. "So when you get her then what? What if she doesn't want to leave? It's been years, man. Things could be different now."

"I know." Slade sighed. "But what belongs to me is mine in life and death."

Killa nodded. "I get that too."

"But to answer your question if she doesn't come, if she wants to stay, I guess I have to wait for next lifetime." He ran his hand down his head. "Nothing will stop us. We will be together eventually."

"Ole romantic ass nigga."

"Fuck you!" Slade laughed nudging him.

Killa looked in the back seat at Audio who was knocked out, mouth open and drool running down his jaw. "Look at this nigga here." He shook his head. "I knew the weed that bitch gave him would have him fucked up. Talking 'bout people following us."

Slade adjusted his mirror so he could see Audio leaning against his window, his tongue hanging out his mouth. "Always wanna get high but can never handle the smoke."

"Even with age he still a big kid," Killa laughed.

"That's what I love about him though," Slade said seriously. "As much as he gets on my nerves sometimes, he lives life hard. Wish I could be like that. Everything with me is a question."

Killa frowned. "Yeah, that little nigga drives you crazy."

"Don't get me wrong. He do irk me sometimes. But he lives his life the way he wants. How can you not admire him for that?" He paused. "We just gotta make sure we protect him. He ain't good enough alone in these streets."

Killa nodded. "So you really don't believe nobody following us?"

Slade shrugged. "If they are let 'em try something. Ain't nothing stopping me from getting to that woman. I just gotta deal with what comes."

CHAPTER TWENTY-FOUR

MAYONI

"Maybe you can go ask Carlton since you fucking him so well?"

Mayoni peeked down the hallway, and watched Farah enter and exit several rooms as she met with members of The Fold. The little meetings lasted no more than five minutes at a time but she wondered what was being said behind her back. She had to get answers. And when Farah exited Nicola's room Mayoni waited for a few moments and rushed inside without knocking.

Nicola was sitting on the side of the bed with her back faced in Mayoni's direction and when she heard her enter she stood up and turned toward her. "What are you doing in here? I want you out."

"Why so mean? We're basically family right?"

"I asked you a question, what are you doing in here?" Nicola backed into her dresser.

Mayoni took a deep breath. "What was Farah talking to you about just now?"

Nicola smiled. "Oh…so that's what this is about? My *personal* conversation with Farah?"

"Well I must say that I am curious." Mayoni sat on her bed. "She held a meeting with everyone but me. Why is that? I'm starting to feel left out of this family."

"You gotta go ask her." Nicola shrugged. "But I do want to know what happened to my carpet! Why is a patch missing?"

Mayoni looked down at it and shrugged. "You asking me?" She pointed to herself. "I mean, maybe you can go ask Carlton since you fucking him so well?"

"You know what, that's exactly what I'm gonna do." She moved toward the door.

"Oh wait...I forgot," Mayoni said pointing at her with her index finger. "Carlton left The Fold. And I hear it's for good too."

Nicola frowned. "No...no he didn't. He wouldn't—
"

"Actually he did and he would." Mayoni giggled. "You may have suckled his dick a few times but when it comes to knowing him inside out you are clueless, bitch." She stood up. "I mean consider it for a minute. How do you think he reacted when I told him I refused to lay with him again after he'd been with you? The man was mad with sadness and left."

"But he'd been with me before."

"And that's why he's gone. He won't do it again. Twice was far enough."

Nicola placed her hand on her belly and gasped softly. After all this time she'd been trying to get with him. To get him to seriously look her way and now she was realizing she'd never have him the way she wanted. "But he said...he said he would let you know that he had chosen me for his right hand. So he couldn't leave. He wouldn't do that without saying goodbye."

Mayoni glared. "Well he lied about that too, bitch! You will always be the next thing to a Giver and nothing more."

Nicola looked at her long and hard. "I don't believe you."

"You don't have—"

"I believe you did something to him." She pointed in Mayoni's face. "I saw how mad you were when you saw him with me."

Mayoni moved closer. "Be careful about spreading lies though. They're bad for your health."

"It's not a lie." She breathed heavily. "I know about your record. And how you killed your last boyfriend." She paused. "I might be almost like a Giver in your mind but I lived in Crescent too! I remember your file, Mayoni. Whenever you can't get your way you attack."

Mayoni cleared her throat. "So what you gonna do? Break a rule and call the police? Remember we are dead."

She moved even closer.

So close their breasts touched.

"But imagine what would happen if what you said were true and I did kill him?" She paused. "What do you think I'd do to a person who had intentions on snitching on me?" She paused. "Be careful, lady. Be very, very careful."

She stormed out.

FARAH

Farah walked into Cutie's room where she was lying face up on the bed, Phoenix on top of her trying to pry between her yellow thighs. "Get out, Phoenix?" Farah said calmly. "It ain't going down tonight."

"Farah, don't!" Cutie yelled.

"Bounce, Phoenix!"

THE FOLD

He said, "Sorry, Farah I was—"

"Just get out!" Farah demanded again. "Now!"

"Yeah whatever. I'll definitely be back." He got out of bed, grabbed his robe, looked back at Cutie and smoothly walked out the door.

"What you doing, Cutie? Having sex in—" Farah squinted and looked at the bruises on her face. "Wait a minute. Did he hit you?" She walked up to her and touched her cheek, only for Cutie to smack her hand off.

Farah wanted to choke the bitch but held back.

"No! He didn't." She paused. "I was just—"

"You can't even come up with a decent story." Farah glared. "But let me help you. The usual lies when a nigga is kicking your ass is that you fell down the stairs. You ran into a wall or—"

"Just stop it! Stop it! Please!" She jumped out of bed and slipped into Phoenix's t-shirt. "You don't understand."

Farah shook her head. "What happened to you? In your life? To make you think shit is sweet?"

"How you pointing the finger at me like Bones not beating you."

Farah squinted. "But I got plans for that."

"So now that you killed my foster mother you want to pretend to be my parent? Is that what this is?"

"I don't want to be anything but my own person! And I didn't kill your mother." Farah said. "If anything your coming here killed her and complicated my life."

Cutie walked to the mirror. "Then don't bother me because I don't want your help anyway. Me and Phoenix are about to get married and —"

"Marriage has no meaning in this house, Cutie. I told you that before. The only thing we do here is settle the flesh. Basically he'll fuck the shit out of you and then leave you the moment you become boring. They all do."

"You don't know him."

"That's where you're wrong. I had a boyfriend just like him and it didn't end good."

Cutie looked down and cried. "You not talking about Slade are you?"

"No...he's the only one who really gets me but we can never be together. That's the way shit is when you're with The Fold and I have to deal with it."

Slowly Farah walked over to her and said, "I'm working out a plan to get you out of this house."

"What about you?"

"I'm going too."

"Can I go with you?"

"No. You'll need to go to another home or maybe a family member." She paused. "You don't know it but everybody, with the exception of a few Givers, have mental issues. So you don't know what happened to Phoenix or what circumstance he was born into and you don't want to. So you have to leave."

Farah said all of that and Cutie only heard one thing. "Getting me out of this house to live with strangers is your answer? Instead of staying with you? But why?"

"Because it's not safe to be with me. I will always be trouble."

Cutie backed away from her toward the door. "But I'm not leaving anywhere without you. And since you don't want me I won't live without him. I can't be alone."

"Are you insane?"

"I'm not going anywhere without Phoenix!" She screamed. "And you can't make me!"

She stormed out of the room and Farah gave chase until she bumped into Bones. Before addressing Farah, he turned around and looked at Cutie running away. "What's wrong with her?"

Farah cleared her throat. "Nothing."

He glared. "Trust. Remember?"

Farah scratched her scalp. "I think her and Phoenix had a fight." She shrugged. "Sometimes I wish you never hooked them up. They're too intense together."

He smiled, having received a believable answer. "Yeah…he has that effect on the ladies." He looked down the hall again and back at her. "She'll pull through and understand how things work here."

"I'm serious, Bones. He's messing with her head and did you see her face?" She forgot he hit her on the regular basis.

His brows rose. "Wait…he hit her?"

"Yes."

Bones looked away, nodded and stared back into Farah's eyes. He himself beat Farah all the time. "Sometimes you have to establish authority. Let these females know who was in charge. I'm sure that's all he was up to."

Farah bit her tongue because she had choice words for him that she decided to keep to herself. "Maybe."

"By the way, I've been looking all over for Carlton. You seen him lately?"

CHAPTER TWENTY-FIVE

FARAH

"It's been a long time and now we're back!"

It was time for pre-hunt night.

They all stood in the front lawn, two black Mercedes Sprinters with tinted windows and opened doors in the driveway awaited them. Farah walked out of the mansion and up to the pack, her tight red pants and black top showcasing her figure. Bones came out behind her, his hand resting in the small of her back as he took her side.

"I won't be going tonight," Bones said to them. "But Farah will ensure that pre-hunt will be a successful one,"

Farah smiled at them all. "It's been a long time and now we're back!"

The crowd erupted in cheers.

"Although blood is the purpose we must be selective." She looked at all of them. "This is still our home and we must be organized savages. Only invite those who are deserving or we'll have to rid ourselves of them." She looked at Cutie. "Where are the invitations?"

Cutie picked up the box and walked them to the center of the lawn. Farah removed one of the invitations, which were black cards with red embossed lettering that included an address. It would be the place that the guest would be picked up and brought back to the house for the party after they were drugged of course.

"These cards should be given to whom we select, but let's make sure that we only choose top notch people. Let them be sexy but above all let them be worth their weight in blood."

Bones smiled. "The Fold!"

Everyone raised a fist in the air.

"Let's hunt!" Farah added.

When she saw Cutie try to ease into the bus she grabbed her by the collar and pulled her back. "Nah, you staying here. So don't even try it."

"But, Farah, I gotta see how they do it!" She paused. "Please."

"Go back in the house!" Farah yelled. "Ain't nobody paying with you. Now!"

Cutie rolled her eyes and stomped inside. When she was gone Farah focused on Bones. His facial expressions were starting to get colder and she felt she didn't know what he would do from one moment to

THE FOLD

the next. It was like there was no soul behind his eyes. "Are you okay? You seem out of it."

"Is this about Dr. Weil being gone again? And me needing medicine?"

"I'm worried about you."

"Don't be. Just play your position and the rest will fall into place." He slapped her ass and walked into the house.

The Fold had been to three clubs that night looking for worthy victims and so far they were coming up short. All hope was mostly lost until they walked into Club Curtains, an upscale spot in D.C., which cost over ten million to build. Once inside it appeared that every sexy man and woman had made a unanimous decision to patronize the same spot.

"Now this is what I'm talking about," Gregory said rubbing his palms together. He placed a hand on Farah's shoulder. "Good decision."

She looked down at his hand. "Get your fucking fingers off me."

He chuckled and looked back at the men. "This is it, fellas. Let's get to it." Slowly he removed his hand, winked and walked inside.

The men of The Fold bopped forward, a stack of cards in their pockets and thoughts of bloodsucking and ass fucking in their minds.

Eve, Denny and Nicola walked behind Farah. For a minute they watched the men hand card after card to every halfway decent woman in sight. Throughout it all, not one man had received an invite.

"Okay, ladies," Farah said. "Seems the fellas are trying to have this night unevenly matched. We need some dudes in the mix."

Denny puckered her lips. "I'm on it." She and Eve switched off and up to a pack of dope boys while Nicola hung behind.

"Why do I get the impression you're leaving?" She asked Farah.

"What you mean?" Farah was shocked. "We just got here."

"No, I mean permanently." She paused. "You doing a lot and I think...I feel..." She moved closer. "Farah, please don't leave if you're thinking about it. We need you, you know that."

"Nicola, everything will happen that needs to happen." Farah smiled. "Now go get us some men for Blood Night. The girls need help."

Nicola smiled sadly and walked off.

When the night trickled down the fellas retreated to the Sprinters, zero cards in hand. Gregory, however, held back and watched Farah who was overseeing the other girls. The possible Givers were in awe of the women dressed in black with red accents that were approaching them.

"You think it's cool that they giving invites to so many dudes?" Gregory questioned. "If you ask me it's too much and Mayoni would never have given so many access. It ain't like ya'll don't like sucking from ladies too. Why have too many niggas if we don't need 'em?" He shrugged.

Farah laughed softly. "You talk to me as if I can forget."

He cleared his throat. "What you talking about?"

"I remember everything you did to me. And when the time is right I'll show you."

He frowned. "Fuck that mean?"

She walked off.

The hallway within the mansion was dark as Farah tiptoed down it. Slowly she used the letter opener in her pocket to pop the lock of a door and push her way inside Dr. Weil's office. It took almost five minutes and she still hadn't found what she was looking for. She knew time was not on her side because not only was Bones always looking for her but lately his obsession with being in the office was borderline psychotic. So he was bound to come back at any second.

After locating the file she was on her way out when Bones walked inside and frowned. Quickly, she hid the file behind her back. "Hey, bae."

"What you doing in here?" He paused and looked around. "And how did you get inside?"

Farah trembled as her mind raced about the best thing to say. "Gregory tried to rape me again," she lied.

"What?"

"Ever since you gave them the okay to disrespect me they do it everyday!" She yelled.

"But—"

"Am I your rider or not?"

"What?" He paused. "Yeah!"

"Then let them niggas know that I belong to you! I'm not feeling safe in our own home and I thought you told me with you in charge I would."

He remained still.

"Now, Bones! Please!"

He looked at her once more and walked out. Farah used the opportunity to escape with the files in her hand.

"No just ask him if he knows anybody who wants to make a little extra money." Farah sat on the edge of her bed.

"Farah, why don't you just leave that place?" Mia asked. "Why do all of this?"

"There's nothing I want more than to bounce. But I gotta take care of them first."

"But why?" Mia continued. "Because if the shoe were on the other foot they wouldn't give a fuck about you."

Farah sighed. "Mia, just call my white daddy and give him the file I faxed to you earlier. Ask if he can find everything I need on that list." She paused. "Please."

"Okay, Farah whatever."

CLICK.

CHAPTER TWENTY-SIX

FARAH

"It's Pre-Shikar and you're asking me about
Carlton?

Pre-Shikar Night had arrived and everyone was excited.

Bones stood next to Farah as he looked out at the twenty-one members that made up The Fold. They were outside the door of the party room, in the hallway and most were more agitated than they had been in the past, under Dr. Weil's leadership, but Farah was the only one who seemed to notice.

"Tonight we prepare for blood night!" Bones said out loud. "And, we have twenty-four Givers ready behind these doors! Make sure you interview those you'd like to stay and get rid of the others you don't. Thank you to everyone."

"Aren't you going to thank me?" Mayoni asked, half drunk. She walked to the front of the crowd. "After all, it was my idea."

Bones nodded. "Yes...thanks to Mayoni." He cleared his throat as Farah gave her a sinister smile. "Now...enjoy. Enjoy them hard. You deserve it."

Farah pushed open the doors and the members piled inside. Once the doors opened they had their pick of the sexiest men and women imaginable. Mayoni, salty as fuck, was about to walk inside when Bones stopped her with a firm hand to the chest.

"What's going on with you?" He closed the door to the room. "Why you acting like a bitch lately?"

She frowned. "What that supposed to mean?"

He looked her up and down. "Look at you, Mayoni. You look a mess and I can smell your pussy from here. Did you even wash your hair?"

She folded her arms across her body. "Wow. So now you disrespect me too."

"Where is Carlton? I've been looking all over for him and nobody seems to have an answer."

"I don't know... why don't you ask Farah." She shrugged.

"Why would I ask Farah when I'm asking you? He's your nigga."

"Because I saw them in the room alone the other day." She paused. "And it looked like they were having a pretty heated conversation too. Maybe she has more information, I don't know. Just guessing."

Bones threw his locks back and scratched his head. "Why would Farah be having a conversation with

Carlton that's heated? They don't have anything in common."

Mayoni shrugged before she moved closer to him. "I don't know about that, Bones, but you know what I want to talk about?" She paused. "How you spend all your time looking at Farah and never considered me as your girl."

"Considered you as my girl?' He chuckled. "Are you okay?"

"And if I'm not? What exactly are you gonna do?"

He frowned. "You know what, I'm done talking to you." He pointed in her face. "The first thing I want you to do is go get cleaned up. Looking how you do right now is a bad representation on The Fold." She walked closer to him and he pushed her away. "Go wash your fucking ass! Now!"

She stared at him for a moment and smiled. "You're right. I've...I've been out of sorts. Let me go shower and come back to the party later. Maybe we can spend a little time alone then? Just me and you?"

Bones nodded.

She left and his eyes remained on her the entire time.

With her gone, Bones entered the party and approached Farah. "When was the last time you've seen Carlton?"

She shook her head. "It's Pre-Shikar and you're asking me about Carlton? Again? When I told you I haven't seen him?"

"Mayoni said you were with him last."

"Mayoni is a liar." She paused. "But forget all of that." She wrapped her arms around his neck and kissed his lips once. "Let's enjoy the scene.

CHAPTER TWENTY-SEVEN

SLADE

"My brothers...where are they?"

Slade pulled up at the rest stop with his brothers fast asleep. He looked over at Killa and nudged his arm. "We here! Get up. Go piss and shit so we can get back on the road."

Killa and Audio roused a little out of their sleep. "Damn, you got here quick." Killa said rubbing his eyes. He looked back at Audio and punched his leg. "Get up, man. You said you had to take a dump earlier so it's time."

"Finally!" Audio clapped his hands, pushed opened the car door and moved into the cool night. The moment the breeze hit his face he felt something was wrong. It was in the air. Across the parking lot, under the cover of the purple sky, he saw headlights on a black Tahoe pointed in their direction.

The same vehicle that had been following them.

"Slade," Audio said under his breath. "Something is...something is up."

Slade looked in the direction Audio was staring into when suddenly bullets came crashing into the car. "RUNNNNNNNNN!" Slade yelled.

He and his brothers went ducking for cover but the bullets came crashing from all angles. Over their heads, around their bodies they flew as the brothers ran inside the rest stop for cover. Hearing the heavy artillery, patrons screamed and grabbed their children trying to get away from the terror that was obviously coming their way.

Four men were busting shot after shot with one idea in mind, to slay the Baker brothers and honor the orders handed down to them by Mayoni. Although years had passed since they been home with The Fold, they never lost contact with who they were, vamps. All three wanted to be with their family after living down south for years. Now freedom from the southern life would forever be held back if they didn't take Slade's head.

Slade, Audio and Killa, out of breath, hid behind the counter of Pepper's Chicken inside the rest stop. It had closed for the night and for now it kept them out of sight. "We have to split up," Slade whispered.

"Why?" Audio asked with wide eyes. "It's best if we—"

THE FOLD

"It's smart so we can shake these dudes. I'm gonna throw them off your tracks."

"Come on, man, don't do this," Audio pled. "I don't have a good feeling about this."

Slade looked at Killa who placed a firm hand on Audio's shoulder. "We gotta go, man," Killa said. " It's time."

"Wait for me to move first." Slade said as he leapt from behind the counter. Two gunmen who were across the empty rest stop gave chase. To get them away from his brothers he exited through the door on the left and ran out back. Luckily someone who had been taking out the trash earlier left the door opened allowing Slade to slip in and his brothers to go free.

Hiding behind tons of flour sitting on a rack, Slade saw one gunman tail him. When they were close, he pushed the rack hard enough to fall on him. With him pinned under the weight, he snatched the weapon from his hand and shot him in the throat.

And then he waited.

For the other one.

Flipping the light switch off he hid for five minutes and saw a shadowy figure enter the doorway.

"Kevin, are you in here?" The gunman asked, his voice quivering. "Kevin, stop—"

Using the gun Slade killed him with a single bullet to the gut. With him down he hopped over the body and re-entered the rest stop. He could faintly hear sirens and knew cops were in route but the last thing he wanted was to be caught or questioned by police. But he couldn't go anywhere without his brothers. The worst of it all was that he was out of bullets.

"Stop right there!" A stranger yelled.

When Slade focused he was able to see the last shooter standing in front of a large window, aiming a gun in his direction.

Slade felt weak.

Where was Audio and Killa?

"My brothers...where are they?"

"It doesn't matter," he said through clenched teeth. "Where are *my* niggas?" As he aimed the gun his hand shivered and Slade felt he would accidently shoot him before doing it on purpose. "You killed them didn't you?"

Slade froze. "I...I—"

"We been watching you for the longest time, nigga. And now it's about to be over. Two fucking years I been looking at the back of your bald head!" He yelled. "AND I'M SICK OF THIS SHIT!"

"Man, I didn't—"

"Shut the fuck up! Just shut up!"

Slade nodded. "You got it, man."

"You're gonna—"

When Slade looked behind the shooter he saw the lights to a Tahoe truck coming full speed ahead. So Slade took one step to the left just as the Tahoe The Fold was driving earlier came crashing into the window, rolling over the shooter in the process. Glass and cement splattered everywhere.

The window of the driver's side rolled down and Audio stuck his head out. "You coming, big bruh or nah?"

CHAPTER TWENTY-EIGHT

FARAH

"I'm still being watched so I can't leave the mansion. But I'm gonna send someone who can."

Farah's eyes flew open when the air had been choked from her lungs. In rage, Bones was on top of her, squeezing her throat with as much pressure as a mad man could possess which in his case was a lot. And then, as if a light flipped on in his mind, he released, crawled off the bed and sat on the chair across from where she lay.

Farah rolled over and coughed.

"Where is that diary?"

She continued to hack, trying to pull air back into her lungs.

"Relax, it wasn't that hard," he paused. "Now where is it?"

"Bones, what's going on?" She coughed again.

"I've been looking for Carlton for days," he said skipping the subject. "He was the closest person I had to a brother." He exhaled. "And now I hear that he's...that something —"

"Bones, what are you telling me?"

"May, she, she basically told me tonight that you killed Carlton."

"Bones, we are supposed to be preparing for blood night. Don't listen to her." Farah sat up and scooted back against the headboard. The room spinning in her vision. That whore had lied on her and she wished her a slow death. "And if he is gone it wasn't me."

"He was Dr. Weil's original pick to run things." He smiled to himself. "He wanted him to handle everything pertaining to The Fold and our business. " He cleared his throat. "But back then he was about Mayoni too much to give him a break."

Farah took a deep breath. "I didn't hurt him. I got no beef with him now or ever."

"Dr. Weil saw something else in me. At least that's what he said. But I think he felt I was cold, and not caring. But I called it ambition."

"Bones, if I could help you, would you take it? With some medicine?"

"I DON'T NEED NO FUCKING DRUGS! SO STOP ASKING ME!" He yelled. "You're spoiled, Farah. And I don't know what I'm gonna do about that."

His eyes were wiled with hate and she didn't feel safe. The longer she stayed around him the worst it got. Now she believed Mia was right to just take her chances and leave. But she knew Bones would find her, along with members of The Fold. Some of which she'd come to care about.

No, she had to stick around. For a little longer anyway.

"Bones, I didn't kill Carlton."

"Who?" He frowned.

"Carlton...you asked me about him and I'm telling you I didn't kill him."

He rose. "So what, I don't give a fuck about that nigga anyway." He skipped the subject again, as if he were bipolar. "If he dead that means he's weak. And I will live forever."

"Well, what exactly did he say?" Farah asked as she sat on the closed toilet seat and talked to her sister on the phone.

"He doesn't want to be involved."

She exhaled. "But did you tell him why I needed his help?"

"I did. And all he told me was that he wasn't about to get any of the drugs on that list for no amount of money." She paused. "What are you gonna do with the drugs anyway?"

"Mia—"

"Fuck it, don't tell me." She paused. "Just know that your white father draws the line at prescription dope fraud when it comes to helping you."

"What am I gonna do?" Farah said to herself.

"You didn't let me finish." Mia yelled. "He didn't want to help but the father who raised you did."

Farah frowned. "You talked to daddy in prison?"

"Yep."

"But calls are recorded. That's dangerous!"

"I visited him, Farah. I'm not stupid."

Farah got up and punched the air happily.

"He gave me the name of the man you have to meet so what you gonna do now?"

"I'm still being watched so I can't leave the mansion. But I'm gonna send someone who can."

CHAPTER TWENTY-NINE

MAYONI

"Everything so far sounds like a colossal fuck up."

M ayoni paced the bar inside the mansion with the phone pressed against her ear. "What are you talking about you missed?" She paused. "And how are all three of them dead but you?"

"I don't know…I mean things got out of hand and I ran." He sighed. "We'd been following them from the moment they left and then when you told us to proceed with the hit, we tried to execute. To be honest I don't know what else you want me to say. The shit didn't work."

"Fuck!" She said to herself. "So where, how can…" She couldn't even get her words straight. When she gave the order to kill Slade to get back at Farah, she hadn't thought about what would happen if they got away. "This is bad. Very bad."

"May, can I come home now?" He paused. "I know we fucked up but it's been two years and I kinda miss being there."

"Yes, I guess so." She rolled her eyes. This dude was useless.

"Can you send money? Because they stole our truck too."

"Stole the truck too?" Her nostrils flared. "How? I mean what the fuck did you do right?" She paused. "Because everything so far sounds like a colossal fuck up."

"I'm sorry, May. The guy with the baldhead was smarter than we thought. What else can I say?"

She sighed deeply. "I'll send money but when you get here come see me first. I want your come back to be a surprise." She paused, knowing that the real plan was to murder his ass the moment he stepped on the mansion's concrete step. "And don't report that truck stolen. We don't want the police in our business."

"Sure, May." He said excitedly.

"Before you go, where do you think they are headed?"

"We fucked up their car pretty bad before they took ours. So if I had my
guess I'd say back to Mississippi to regroup. Don't worry."

CHAPTER THIRTY

SLADE

"Stop fucking around. What's the address man?"

Slade, Audio and Killa cruised down the street only eighty miles from D.C. Exhausted; Slade took a deep breath before turning to Audio. "Okay man, we almost in D.C. so what's the address?"

Audio, who sat in the passenger seat rubbed his eyes. The shoot out took all the energy from him and he needed a quick nap. "Um...it's...I think it's..."

"What is it?"

"Wait, man, I...I'm trying to think."

Slade frowned. "You trying to think? Are you serious? Stop fucking around. What's the address man?"

"Wait a minute," he yawned. "I'm trying to remember."

"Audio, please tell me we didn't come all this way only for you not to know where we going." Killa interjected. "Because that's the only reason you here remember. You threw up in our face that you had the drop on her house. So give it to us."

"Don't get me wrong, I been to her crib the one time but it's been a minute."

Slade pulled the car over and parked. This could not be happening. "Audio, don't do this to me."

Audio scratched his head. "I...I can't remember, man. I'm sorry, big bro."

"Wait...you're serious?"

Silence.

Wanting to kill Audio, Slade pushed the car door open and leaned against it instead. There was no use in hurting him, although he wanted to. Running his hand down his face he screamed into his palms. First his baby's mother tried to off his son, then they were robbed on the side of the road, next they were shot at while at a rest stop and now he was learning that all of that, everything, would be for nothing."

Killa stepped out the car, walked toward Slade and placed his hand on his shoulder. "Want me to kill him?"

Slade smiled for a second. "Nah, it ain't even worth it."

Killa nodded and stuffed his hands into his jean pockets. "I know...but what you wanna do?"

"I gotta let her go, man. It's like everything is trying to stop me from getting back to shawty. Maybe it's for the best."

"Either that or the universe is trying to make you prove how much you want her." He pointed at her. "I guess it's all in how you look at it."

Slade shook his head.

"I got it!" Audio said tapping the steering wheel.

Slade and Killa turned around and focused on the truck. Looking at Audio through the opened window, they waited for whatever debacle he was about to hit them with.

"The GPS!" Audio said excitedly.

"What you talking about?" Slade frowned.

"They got one in here. Maybe they put their address in the system and stored it."

Slade looked at Killa.

"Nah, they wouldn't be that stupid," Killa said. They all stared at one another trying to consider the possibility. "Or would they?" He continued.

Audio pressed a button and activated the GPS while Slade and Killa waited with baited breath. After a few more presses something happened.

"Son!" Audio said looking at his brothers with wide eyes. "This shit actually says The Fold. These niggas dumb as fuck!"

Slade, Killa and Audio cheered happily.

CHAPTER THIRTY-ONE

BONES

"If you want me to respect you then be honest, bitch."

Farah went in and out of each member's room, with Nicola right behind her holding a bag full of meds that were good enough for a few months. Nicola had met with Mia earlier to secure the medicine and now Farah was distributing it to the members who were willing to use it with Dr. Weil gone.

As she did her good deed, she didn't realize Bones was watching her down the hallway from afar. "What is she up to?" Bones asked himself.

Mayoni walked up behind him. "What you doing?"

"You lied. Farah would never have killed Carlton."

She walked in front of him. "She did! She's lying and—"

"Cut the shit!" Bones snapped. "If you want me to respect you then be honest, bitch."

"I want more than for you to respect me." She exhaled.

"What you talking about?"

"I chose wrong, Bones. I assumed Carlton was as strong as you and he wasn't. It's always been you, Bones. Always been about you but there always seemed to be another bitch waiting."

His brows lowered. "Did you kill Carlton?"

"If it puts me closer to you, would you blame me?"

His dick jumped.

All he ever wanted was a woman who realized his strength and power. Mayoni wasn't as sexy as Farah but she recognized a real nigga when she saw one. And for him that meant more these days. "If you want me, prove your loyalty."

"Okay…" She took a deep breath. "I will tell you why I killed Carlton."

"So you did kill Carlton?"

She nodded.

Bones adjusted in place. "I'm listening."

"I killed him because he was supposed to kill Slade and didn't."

Bones glared.

His nostrils flared.

His temperature rose.

Suddenly in his warped mind everything made sense. Farah didn't submit to his will because Slade was still alive. "As I recall, I asked you both to murder him. And you forbade me by leaving that nigga alive? When you knew he was my worst enemy because he wanted my bitch?" He quickly squeezed her throat, limiting her breath. "It was Carlton."

"And how do I know I can believe you now?"

She raised one hand. "Because I cut my wrist so you can drink my blood to your fill. You can either take my life or take me to the hospital when you're done. Either way, it was an honor to serve you."

Bones grabbed her wrist and sucked deeply until Mayoni passed out.

BONES

Swanson was on his way back into the party when Bones approached him, the corners of his mouth still covered with Mayoni's blood. He grabbed him by the arm and led him a few feet away from the door.

"Slade is alive," Bones whispered.

"Wait, you mean, that dude Farah dealt with before—"

"Yeah, that mothafucka!" He said cutting him off. "He's alive!"

Swanson ran his hand down his face. "Damn, boss, I'm sorry. So what you gonna do?"

"I'm gonna burn this place down, literally." He paced a little in place. "If I do will you stand by me?" He pointed at him.

"Yes!"

"But where are we gonna live?"

"I'll come up with a plan." He paused. "What about if I have to kill Farah?"

"You already know it," he paused. "I'm still with you. Especially after that last time when—"

"When you tried to rape her again and I caught your ass?" Bones asked through clenched teeth. He pointed at him. "Don't think I forgot about that. Just decided maybe she ain't the girl for me after all." He ran his hand down his face. "Anyway be ready when it's time. Let Gregory know too."

"I will."

It was official Shikar.

The guests for part two of the party were selected to give blood and it was time. In their feeble minds they were coming to a party but when the night was said and done they would all be a few pints of blood lighter.

To enhance the moment, all had been given black colored ecstasy pills and were already in the mood for anything. And although the room was filled, many of them who were picked at the club were subsequently denied entry on the bus leading to the mansion.

The reasons were many.

One chick had five kids and was pregnant with her sixth. Another girl was discovered to have herpes and one dude had slept with a transsexual. Although his sexual preference had nothing to do with his blood, it was learned that one of his sleeping partners was a whore with hepatitis.

The Fold thought about everything to make sure blood night was enjoyable and safe.

Earlier, before the ecstasy, a powerful sleep suppressant was given to them all by way of a grape flavored Kool-Aid. Once they were knocked out, all were given HIV tests. Those who were positive, and

THE FOLD

there were two, were taken while sleep and dropped off at the closest bus station.

They would be of no use to The Fold.

And now, it was time to drink blood, fuck and party.

Nicola was riding a Giver she invited in the middle of the floor. They weren't the only two or three having sex because not a man or woman in The Fold was shy. When he was about to cum, she removed a gold razor from the pocket of her bra and slit into the flesh of his shoulder.

"Ouch!" he yelled. "What the fuck was that?" He looked down and saw his own blood. "What you just do?"

She smiled, sucked his blood and looked at him. "Just go with it. It'll be worth your while I promise. You never met a bitch like me."

He stared at her for a moment but the E had him feeling adventurous. "Fuck it! Do what you gotta do."

She smiled and slid her tongue around the brown and red flesh oozing with more blood, all while continuing to fuck him hard while on top of him. He had never experienced anything so sexual in all his life.

Eve and Denny were fucking the dog shit out of a red bone from New York. The meaty part of Eve's pussy rubbed against the Giver's tongue and lips while Denny sucked his dick to an extreme thickness. Eve already came twice and was working on her third, which was dangerously close.

"Damn this shit can't be real," the Giver said. "It feels too good. Who are ya'll? What is this place? And why can't I remember getting here?"

"Don't worry about who we are," Denny said. "Worry about what we gonna do to you." Her pussy juiced up at the way she was servicing him.

"Say no more. You can—"

"Ouch!" He yelled pushing Eve off of his face. "What was that?" He looked down at his dick and moved his balls to see what was wrong.

"I'm sorry, I think I pulled a hair or something," Denny said. "But don't worry about it."

"Yeah, let me take care of that with my homie," Eve said. "The last thing we want is you being in pain."

Before he could dispute, they took turns sucking the blood pouring out of the secret gash under his balls. Years of sucking and cutting made them more skillful than a surgeon and the ladies, like the others, were strategic in their approach. Certain cuts yielded more blood and members of The Fold knew them all.

Farah walked into a sea of Vamps and Givers. The moment her yellow well manicured toes hit the carpet, all present people gave her their undivided attention. Her beauty in itself was filling to the eyes as people wondered how she tasted and smelled.

Bones, who had learned that Slade was still alive, observed her from a far, hate in his heart because he realized she would never be his, no matter how much he loved her or beat her.

His eyes were red from having his fill of blood while Mayoni was in the room recovering. Looking at him, and thinking he wanted a show, she lowered her body and laid face up on the floor. Besides, she needed satisfaction and she needed it now. Four members of The Fold and a few Givers covered her body with their own; their lips still red with blood.

One beautiful Giver removed Farah's left breast and sucked her nipple while another took to her right. Two givers raised the dress and licked her pussy until she tingled all over. She was in extreme ecstasy and needed the mental break like yesterday and finally.

For a moment she imagined she was with Slade and she could actually feel his tongue coursing the flesh of her body. And just as she came into Nicola's mouth, when she opened her eyes Bones was looking down at her with disdain.

Gregory was fucking a Giver so hard from the back her legs quivered. Unlike other Givers at the party she wasn't having a good time. He was too rough and she

THE FOLD

was more afraid than anything. She even tried to leave but he yanked her hair and yelled, "Take this dick, bitch! Or I'ma make you-"

Before she knew it, her period had come down and members of the Fold saw it from a far. Seeing the red liquid flowing freely, slowly they rose and rushed toward her, each trying to suck the blood flowing between her legs. Suddenly the woman who was once in pain was now aroused as Phoenix, Gregory, Swanson and Wesley sucked her pussy until her struggles were over.

Her body trembled.

Her toes curled.

And her pressure rose, causing her more pleasure as she was brought to an orgasm.

Everybody in the mansion was having a good time.

All except one.

Bones.

Even Cutie managed to peek in and witness the scene. It was just like she imagined from the diary only better.

Sexual.

Hot.

Bloody.

Still, the moment Farah spotted her, she jumped up.

CHAPTER THIRTY-TWO

FARAH

"Let me help you, Bones. Please. I have the ability
to do it now."

Farah walked through the doors and into the
hallway. But where was Cutie?"

"Cutie! I'm gonna fuck you up when I find you!"
She continued to walk down the hall. "Cutie!" She
trekked forward like a mother wanting to explain to
her child what she'd just seen. "You better come here
or—"

Her hunt for Cutie ended abruptly when suddenly
she was struck over the back of the head with a blunt
object, falling face first to the cool black marble.

Farah woke up to a throbbing headache. When she
opened her eyes Wesley, Gregory and Swanson were
surrounding her. Bones in the middle of it all. They
were in her room and she was tied to a wooden chair.

"Bones, what are you doing? I —"

"Where is Slade?"

"Slade?" Her heart rate increased upon hearing his name. "I don't know what you talking —"

Bones smacked her hard. "Is he alive?"

"Bones, I don't —"

He slapped her on the other side of her face. "Don't make me punch you next, bitch. Is he alive?"

"Okay, okay, but, Bones, I, I wanna talk to you first."

"'Bout what?"

She took a deep breath. "You have been coming undone for a while now. And it's not your fault." She paused. "It's because without the medicine you're not the same, so let me help you, Bones. Please. I have the ability to do it now."

He slapped her again and her gaze fell downward. Slowly she raised her head and looked at him. "I'm warning you." She paused. "Don't do that again."

He punched her and she looked at the men behind Bones and nodded. Suddenly, Swanson stole Bones in the mouth, knocking him to the ground. Bones was caught off guard so much he thought something fell from the ceiling.

"Fuck is you doing?" Gregory asked Swanson, before he knocked him down also.

With the two men on the floor, Wesley untied Farah and handed her the gun in his waist. Slowly she walked toward Gregory and shot him in the dick without any questions asked. When he yelled she shot him in the face too. "I knew I'd look down on your corpse." She spit on Gregory before moving to Bones.

"So this is what my men do? Take the side of a traitor?" Bones yelled at them. "I thought you didn't fuck with her?" He asked Swanson. "What about all that shit earlier?"

"That was all a ruse, man. I came to Farah the day you saw us in the hallway covered in blood and said I was sorry when I learned she was getting medicine. You didn't want to medicate us and I'm feeling a little better. I don't want to be the monster I can be. And I can't have you burning down the mansion. I'm sorry."

"But where did all the blood come from?"

"I cut myself."

Bones gritted his teeth. "I can't believe this shit."

"I gave you every opportunity to do right," Farah said to Bones. "And you didn't accept any of them."

He took a deep breath. "Before you kill me answer me this. Did you ever give a fuck about—"

BOOM!

She shot him in the mouth. "I'm sick of your voice. Die today, bitch! I don't fuck with weak niggas."

Farah, Swanson and Wesley moved toward Mayoni's room eager to rid The Fold of all snakes and possible traitors. But when they arrived they saw her sitting up against the head post, blood drained from her body, skin ash grey.

After holding Swanson and Wesley to secrecy that Bones, Gregory and Mayoni were dead, Farah sent them back to the party to act normal. She herself needed time to plan her exit strategy because she knew they wouldn't want her leaving even though the real threats were gone. She was almost to her room when she saw Slade, Audio and Killa standing in the foyer.

THE FOLD

She blinked a few times.

"Am I dreaming?" She said to herself.

"Nah, bae," Slade said. "It's me and I'm here."

She passed out.

Farah slowly opened her eyes and blinked three times to clear her vision. Each time Slade was staring her down and she realized she wasn't dreaming. Beyond ecstatic, she leapt up and hugged him tightly.

"My God, how did you...I don't understand." She kissed him so many times she couldn't speak.

"Took me a minute but I'm here now," Slade said. "I guess you can say a nigga came back for you."

"But...how?"

"Lets just say I went through a lot to find what's mine."

"But why?" She paused. "After all this time I figured you'd gone on with your life."

He smiled and wiped her hair behind her ear. "I'm here because when I look at you I see my reflection."

She hugged him again and looked around. Her eyes widened when she realized they'd taken her to Dr. Weil's room. When she looked to the right she saw Audio and Killa staring her down.

"Can I be with you alone, Slade?" She asked. "Without your brothers?"

"Ain't no problem with me," Audio said. "Sounded like folks were fucking at a party down the hallway so I figure we could slide in there and give you some privacy in here if you don't mind. That way everybody can have a little fun."

"NO!" Farah jumped off the bed. "I mean...no. They don't know who you are." She walked to a side door and opened it. "This is Nicola's room. Wait in there."

Killa shrugged but Audio was heated as they moved inside. Then she closed the door, turned around and looked up at Slade. "I miss you." He exhaled. "I want you to go back with me. Down south."

"Yes."

He walked over to her and picked her up. Slowly he carried her to the bed and for a second he looked down at her and she up at him. And then something clicked. They began ripping each others clothes off like mad people. This moment wasn't about lovemaking.

This was about straight fucking. They didn't stop until they snatched and pulled off everything, Farah's naked body on top of his.

He winked.

She smiled.

And then he filled her with a gut full of dick. Feeling too good for words, Farah bit down on her bottom lip and moved up and down his chocolate pole. Her pussy was already moist when she saw him but now she was dripping wet, cream rolling down his stick like caramel on an apple.

"Fuck!" he moaned. "This shit still right." He paused. "After all this time."

"I love you, Slade. You have no idea how much I've missed you and how much I've thought about you. I thought you...I thought you gave up on me."

Her seriousness caught him off guard. "I love you too, beautiful. Why else would I be here? And I could never give up on you."

Slowly he moved in and out of her.

"And I'm ready to be your wife. That is if you'll have me."

They continued to explore each other as if it were the first time. *The only thing that would make this better is if I could taste you.* She thought.

Like he read her mind he said, "Do what you wanna."

Farah reached over to the dresser, grabbed a gold razor and cut into the chocolate flesh of his skin until she reached the pink center and a red well of blood.

When the liquid oozed outward she lapped it up slowly, causing Slade's dick to get harder with the pain and pleasure he was experiencing. And then he moaned, "Fuck!" As she sucked him until the roof of her mouth stung. "That feels so good." He paused and came inside of her. "Damn, that shit was right," he said slapping her ass. "Sorry it was so quick but it's been so long."

"It was even better to me." She rolled back on top of him. "So tell me, Slade. What have you been doing?"

He sighed. "I got a son now."

Her stomach turned and ached. "Oh...that's—" She sat next to him. Her stomach hurt and she felt gut punched.

"I don't love her, Farah. And she knows it. That's why I'm here."

A single tear fell from her eyes and he kissed it away. "What about me? I mean, where does my life fit in all of this? You already have a family. What you gonna do with an extra problem like me?"

"Farah, I didn't come all this way to play no games with your heart or mind. I came to talk to you. To get you and take you back with me. And anybody who got a problem with that, including my son's mother, can kill themselves and I'll help them along the way." He paused. "The only thing you need to be telling me is if you're coming with me or not."

"I'm ready, Slade, so let me let my friends know." She kissed him. "But the answer is and will always be…yes."

CHAPTER THIRTY-THREE

FARAH

"So I'm asking you not to leave. Please."

Nicola and Zashay looked at Farah as if she were crazy upon hearing the devastating news. "I'm not understanding. You...can't leave us, Farah," Nicola pleaded. "Why would you even say this now with everything going on?"

They were standing outside in the hallway next to the orgy that was taking place. "I'm sorry but I have to go."

"But Bones and Dr. Weil are gone," Nicola said. "And if what you say is true, so is Mayoni and Carlton. That means we are without any leadership if you go. Please, Farah. If you care about us you wouldn't leave like this."

"She's right, Farah," Zashay added. "Nicola put me onto everything going on and as much as we beef I care about you. And we do need you."

"But I thought you hated me."

"I hated myself for caring about the woman the love of my life wanted," Zashay paused. "But that isn't a problem anymore now is it? The nigga is dead and I'm glad. You are the only one thinking clearly now."

Farah sighed. "Slade is here."

Both girls got excited.

"Oh my God!" Nicola yelled. "Good for you, Farah!"

"Now let us meet the man who is almost like a legend around here."

"But it's not good. He's here to take me away." She paused. "To take me home."

Nicola sighed deeply, where she was almost brought to tears. "Farah, if he loves you he would not do that." Nicola pointed at the floor. "This is your home."

"She's right," Zashay said. "You are a vamp. And vamps need blood and we need you. The little pills you gave us won't change that."

Slade, Audio and Killa stood in front of Farah in the middle of Dr. Weil's office where they just made love, and now she was having to deliver bad news. Nicola and Zashay stood behind her.

"Am I missing something?" Slade asked. "One minute you say you wanna leave with me and the next…"

"I *do* want to leave with you." She paused. "It's just that I can't go now."

"See that's the thing, Farah. It's either now or never."

"Slade, maybe you can stay here," Farah suggested. "It's enough room for you. You'll love it here with a little time."

Audio rubbed his hands together and eyed Zashay and Nicola. "Now that I think about it, your friends are looking hella sweet, Farah." Audio rubbed his hands together again. "I can definitely learn to love it here."

"Shut the fuck up!" Slade said to him before turning back around and looking at Farah. "Listen, I'm not leaving here without you. I didn't come this far for nothing."

"Slade, baby, the love of my life." She grabbed his hands. "I can't leave my family."

"Your family? You don't share no blood with these niggas." He frowned.

"Well technically she does," Audio said.

Slade glared.

"Farah, what about me? Ain't I family too?" His nostrils flared. "Don't you wanna finally see what we can be? Together. This is what it's always been about. Getting back to *us*."

"I want nothing more." She hugged him. "So I'm asking you not to leave." She separated from him. "Please."

"You know what, fuck all that." He looked at her hard and picked her up, before tossing her over his shoulder, quickly moving toward the exit.

"Let her go!" Nicola yelled.

"Stop!" Zashay screamed. "Put her down!"

When Slade made it out of the mansion with Farah still hung over his shoulder like a fresh t-shirt, his brothers behind him, he heard the sound of many guns cocking. Slowly he turned around and eight barrels were aimed at him.

All fully loaded.

"Let her go," Swanson warned. "Now."

Slade glared. "Ya'll niggas gonna have to shoot cause I'm not putting my bitch down. Fuck that shit."

"So be it then, big country," Swanson and the others were about to blast him off the planet.

"WAIT!" Farah yelled. "Don't shoot him, Swanson. Please. I love him and I'm begging you."

Swanson continued to aim.

"Put your guns down!" Farah yelled to The Fold. "Now!"

Slowly they lowered their weapons.

"Slade, please let me go," she said softly.

"Farah—"

"Slade, if you love me you'd do what I'm asking." She paused. "Please."

Slowly he released her to stand on her feet. Looking up at him she said, "I can't leave with you right now. I wish I could but now is not the best time."

"Like I said it's now or never," he said.

She dropped to her knees and held onto his pants. "Then let it be now."

He looked around and sighed deeply. "Get up, Farah." He helped her to her feet.

"Stay, Slade. Stay right here with me."

Slade looked at her and then the members of The Fold. This wasn't his kind of place and as far as he was concerned it never would be. Just then the doors opened again and Cutie bolted out. The moment she laid eyes on him she knew who he was and she fell in love as if he belonged to her. Violating his space immediately, she ran up to him and hugged him tightly. "Slade, it's really you! I can't believe it."

"Cutie, go back in the house," Farah demanded.

"But it's Slade!"

"GO NOW!" Farah yelled. "THIS IS SERIOUS!"

Slowly she pulled herself away from him. "Okay. It was nice meeting you."

Slade focused on Farah and touched her face. "If you don't leave with me now, I guess you're saying that it's over. Is that what you want?"

"Please don't. I can't...I just..."

"Goodbye, Farah Cotton."

"Slade, please!"

He continued to walk away, his brothers behind him.

"Slade, no!" She screamed again. "Please don't GOOOOOOOOO!"

EPILOGUE

ONE YEAR LATER

Farah sat on a red and gold kings chair in the party room. It was the first hunt since last year when Slade showed up at the mansion and she missed him daily although it was of no use. He made his decision and she was stuck with starting a life without him. It was as if someone she loved died everyday and she was forced to relive the hateful moment repeatedly.

As she looked down at the bloodsucking and fucking going on around her, she didn't want to participate at the moment. Her mind was elsewhere.

Don't get her twisted.

Every day a willing participant shared her bed and gave of their sweet blood freely but she was bored and alone, kicking all willing Givers out just to think about Slade when they got too emotional or wanted more from The Fold's new boss. She kept them prosperous and mentally sane…well, a little anyway.

"Farah, you seem sad," Zashay said standing next to her. "I mean, look around. We are richer and more powerful than ever and we owe it all to you. Be happy about it because I am."

"I...I guess. I don't feel well though." She paused. "Sorry."

"You need blood." She paused. "Maybe the Giver I vetted for you will be a match."

"I'm—"

"He's in your room."

"What the fuck are you doing? Givers aren't allowed in our private quarters."

Zashay extended her hand. "Just come with me."

Farah sighed but to get her out of her face she walked away with her. Not feeling like any of it, once she made it to her room her heart rocked when she saw Slade standing in the middle of the floor waiting.

Farah looked back at Zashay excitedly. "Enjoy," she said before winking and walking out.

"Slade, I don't understand," she ran up to him. "Does this mean you'll stay?"

"It means I'm not leaving you. And if you here, guess I'm here too." He wrapped his arms around her waist and kissed her long and hard. "Oh, and I brought Audio with me. I think he joined the little party you were having down the hallway. He missed last years and wasn't interested in missing out again. Hope you don't mind."

"What about your baby? Your son? I don't want to separate you from him."

"Once a month I will visit and send money to make sure he's good. He will always be safe."

She jumped in his arms and he carried her to bed. She pulled the drawer open and grabbed a gold razor. "Can I make you famous?" She asked.

"Go ahead, mama," he winked. "Do your thing."

A FEW DAYS LATER

Phoenix walked toward Cutie's room preparing to try and seduce her again. Lately since Slade and Audio were in the house she was interested in writing and reading her books, something that Slade said she would be good at. Although she said no many times, when she knocked on the door he was surprised to see her sitting in the middle of the bed.

No TV.

No radio.

Just sitting.

THE FOLD

"You called me in here so what's up?"

"Got tired of saying no to you," she tapped the bed. "Come inside."

He approached and the moment they were face to face, she got off the bed and slapped him. "What the fuck?" He held onto his face.

"Aw...I'm sorry," she said in a sad tone. "I didn't mean to hurt you. It's just that I love you so much and you don't love me like I do you."

He frowned. "What is this?"

She slapped him again.

He was about to steal her in the jaw when Audio stepped out of the bathroom. "You don't wanna do that, bruh." He was filing his nails. "Go 'head and let shawty do her thing."

On that note Cutie slapped, kicked and even bit almost every part of his body. She didn't let up until she was tired. When she was done he said, "You're gonna wish you didn't do this."

Audio stepped closer. "Doubt that very much, homie. Get to moving."

Farah was lying up under Slade watching TV when the phone rang. When she picked up her cell she saw it was Mia.

"What you doing?" Mia asked frantically. "I gotta talk to you about something. Are you alone?"

Farah sat up. "What is it? You're scaring me."

"Daddy got put into the SHU (Security Housing Unit) the other day."

"For what?"

"Beating up the inmate who connected you with them drugs."

"But why? He's been looking out. Because of him my people stay medicated."

"Farah them drugs ain't real. They are just different placebo versions of the same meds. So that means this whole year you been paying this nigga thousands for sugar pills."

Farah sat up straight. "But how he know?"

"He was bragging around the prison and daddy overheard him." She paused. "But how they been acting? Do they seem fine?"

Farah thought about the strange blood she'd been seeing around the house, in areas they didn't drink. She thought about the strange articles of clothing she'd find in the lawn or backyard and the I.D.'s that didn't belong to anyone in the group, or the Givers. She even recalled walking past secret conversations that would stop when Farah, the boss, would walk by.

"Farah, how have things been?" Mia asked again. "I mean...maybe they don't need the drugs if things are fine."

"Yeah, maybe you're right."

Suddenly she heard sirens nearing the mansion. When she leapt up and ran outside she saw cops covering the front lawn. Members of The Fold stepped outside of the mansion, along with Slade, Audio and Cutie to see what was going on. Although they were all running from one thing or another, they definitely had legit paperwork that would pass through any scrutiny from the police, but still, no one wanted them there.

One of the policemen walked up to her. "Are you the homeowner?"

She crossed her arms over her chest. "What's going on?"

"I'll take that as a yes."

"You can take it however you want."

He smiled. "Well we're looking for three young ladies who went missing from a nightclub last week."

"What that got to do with us, officer?" Slade asked.

He looked up at him. "A lot. For starters the last call that pinged from one of the girl's cell phone's at this location. So, I guess we got some questions for you and everyone who lives here."

CHARACTER KEY

<u>THE COTTONS</u>

Farah Cotton
Farah hated her lighter skin when she was younger due to every member in her family being dark. As she got older she became arrogant about her complexion believing it gave her privileges. With time her perspective changed. Born with Porphyria, which causes blemishes when she's stressed she drinks blood to ease her pain. We later learned that Ashur, the man she thought was her father was not. Instead it was Jay, her Physical Education teacher in high school.

Shadow Cotton
Shadow is Farah's brother.

Mia Cotton
Mia is Farah's older sister. Had issues with her weight and is a master plan creator.

Chloe Cotton
Chloe is Farah's youngest sister who died in a car accident in which her boyfriend, Audio Baker was also present. We learned it was because Theo Cunningham, the boy the Cottons tormented in the beginning of Redbone, ran her off the road. Chloe later died.

Brownie Cotton
Brownie was Farah's mother. Throughout Farah's life Brownie tormented her because of her lighter skin. Brownie was later murdered by Theo but finished off by Farah.

Ashur Cotton

Ashur, a closeted homosexual, is Mia, Shadow and Chloe's birth father. For years Farah thought he was her birth father despite her light skin. Ashur went to prison for murdering a family in broad daylight at the bus stop.

Elise Gill

Elise Gill, who also suffers from porphyria, is Brownie's mother. She had Brownie at 12 years old. She doesn't wash because household products exacerbate her condition. She is murdered.

THE BAKER BOYS

Slade Baker
Slade is the love of Farah's life. He is very strong and the oldest of the brothers in his family.

Audio Baker
Audio is the youngest brother of the Bakers. He's hot headed and a loose cannon.

Major Baker
Major is also Slade's brother. He sold weed as a kid.

Brian 'Killa' Baker
Killa is Slade's brother. Gambles heavily and enjoys weapons. He learns to always examine the eyes to see the truth versus what they say.

Knox Baker
Knox is Slade's brother. He robbed houses as a kid and ran from Mississippi with the evidence necessary to keep his family out of prison. Farah killed him in her house.

Judge
Judge is the Baker Boys cousin. He killed a lot of people. He's 6 feet tall and ugly as a rhino. His brother is Grant.

Grant
Grant is the Baker Boys cousin He killed a lot of people. He's 5'5" tall, makes the decisions for his brother Judge. Grant wears a stiff smile at all times and he enjoys killing.

THE FOLD

Bones
Bones is second in charge of The Fold. Responsible for keeping things ticking. He's obsessed with Farah Cotton and was a former patient at Crescent Falls Mental Institution. Has long neat dreadlocks running down his back. Loves inflicting pain for sexual gratification

Mayoni
Mayoni is a member of The Fold and responsible for bringing Farah into the group. She's beautiful, Asian and has brown hair. Also a former patient at Crescent Falls Mental Institution.

Carlton
Carlton is a member of The Fold and Mayoni's boyfriend. Carlton has been shaking people for years. The tip of his nose was shot off and he's a former patient at Crescent Falls Mental Institution.

Zashay
Zashay has Munchausen syndrome. Was dating Bones and is a former patient at Crescent Falls Mental Institution.

Nicola
Nicola is a former patient at Crescent Falls Mental Institution.

Denny
Denny is a former patient at Crescent Falls Mental Institution.

Eve

Eve is a former patient at Crescent Falls Mental Institution.

Phoenix
Phoenix is a former patient at Crescent Falls Mental Institution.

Wesley
Wesley is a former patient at Crescent Falls Mental Institution.

Gregory
Gregory is a former patient at Crescent Falls Mental Institution.

Swanson
Swanson is a former patient at Crescent Falls Mental Institution.

Vivica
Vivica is a former patient at Crescent Falls Mental Institution.

Lootz
Lootz is a former patient at Crescent Falls Mental Institution. He was murdered.

Dr. Weil
Dr. Weil is the leader of The Fold. Ten years back he was in charge of Crescent Falls, a mental institution, whose patients were tortured and castrated because they complained about the conditions of this facility. Dr. Weil tried to hold meetings with family members to advise of the conditions but nothing changed. So on Christmas Eve Dr. Weil released 13 patients who were in for treatable illnesses or sexual deviances. He injected the others with anesthesia and set Crescent

Falls on fire. The remaining members make up The Fold.

TWO MEMBERS MISSING FROM THE ORIGINAL THIRTEEEN – CUTIE'S FRIEND WAS ONE.

OTHER CHARACTERS

Theo Cunningham

Theo was kicked in penis by Farah and her siblings as a child. His mother Dinette was killed by Mia and Shadow. He later killed Brownie and Chloe. He also showed Slade proof that she killed his brother Knox.

Sheriff Kramer

Sheriff Kramer deputized the Baker Boys to help remove a motorcycle club called the *Killer Bees* out of town. Things were great until an official police killed another officer while trying to take down the last member. Instead of admitting guilt, Sheriff Kramer turned on the Baker Boys and lied, saying they were responsible. But Knox secretly recorded the initial meeting on his cell phone from where he solicited their help.

Tornado

Tornado was murdered by Slade in the hallway of Platinum Lofts. He was arrested for Tornado's death.

Willie

Willie is Randy's father who was angry that he took over his drug business while he was in prison and wasn't willing to turn it back over upon his release. He later orchestrated his own son's murder.

The Cartel Publications Order Form

www.thecartelpublications.com

Inmates **ONLY** receive novels for $10.00 per book.

(Mail Order **MUST** come from inmate directly to receive discount)

Shyt List 1	_____	$15.00
Shyt List 2	_____	$15.00
Shyt List 3	_____	$15.00
Shyt List 4	_____	$15.00
Shyt List 5	_____	$15.00
Pitbulls In A Skirt	_____	$15.00
Pitbulls In A Skirt 2	_____	$15.00
Pitbulls In A Skirt 3	_____	$15.00
Pitbulls In A Skirt 4	_____	$15.00
Pitbulls In A Skirt 5	_____	$15.00
Victoria's Secret	_____	$15.00
Poison 1	_____	$15.00
Poison 2	_____	$15.00
Hell Razor Honeys	_____	$15.00
Hell Razor Honeys 2	_____	$15.00
A Hustler's Son	_____	$15.00
A Hustler's Son 2	_____	$15.00
Black and Ugly	_____	$15.00
Black and Ugly As Ever	_____	$15.00
Year Of The Crackmom	_____	$15.00
Deadheads	_____	$15.00
The Face That Launched A	_____	$15.00
Thousand Bullets		
The Unusual Suspects	_____	$15.00
Miss Wayne & The Queens of DC	_____	$15.00
Paid In Blood (eBook Only)	_____	$15.00
Raunchy	_____	$15.00
Raunchy 2	_____	$15.00
Raunchy 3	_____	$15.00
Mad Maxxx	_____	$15.00
Quita's Dayscare Center	_____	$15.00
Quita's Dayscare Center 2	_____	$15.00
Pretty Kings	_____	$15.00
Pretty Kings 2	_____	$15.00
Pretty Kings 3	_____	$15.00
Pretty Kings 4	_____	$15.00
Silence Of The Nine	_____	$15.00
Silence Of The Nine 2	_____	$15.00
Prison Throne	_____	$15.00
Drunk & Hot Girls	_____	$15.00
Hersband Material	_____	$15.00
The End: How To Write A	_____	$15.00
Bestselling Novel In 30 Days (Non-Fiction Guide)		
Upscale Kittens	_____	$15.00
Wake & Bake Boys	_____	$15.00
Young & Dumb	_____	$15.00
Young & Dumb 2:	_____	$15.00
Tranny 911	_____	$15.00
Tranny 911: Dixie's Rise	_____	$15.00
First Comes Love, Then Comes Murder	_____	$15.00

296   ***THE FOLD***

Luxury Tax	_____	$15.00
The Lying King	_____	$15.00
Crazy Kind Of Love	_____	$15.00
And They Call Me God	_____	$15.00
The Ungrateful Bastards	_____	$15.00
Lipstick Dom	_____	$15.00
A School of Dolls	_____	$15.00
Hoetic Justice	_____	$15.00
KALI: Raunchy Relived	_____	$15.00
Skeezers	_____	$15.00
You Kissed Me, Now I Own You	_____	$15.00
Nefarious	_____	$15.00
Redbone 3: The Rise of The Fold	_____	$15.00
The Fold	_____	$15.00
Clown Niggas	_____	$15.00
The One You Shouldn't Trust	_____	$15.00
The WHORE The Wind		
Blew My Way	_____	$15.00

(**Redbone 1** & **2** are **NOT** Cartel Publications novels and if **ordered** the cost is **FULL** price of $15.00 **each**. **No Exceptions**.)

Please add $5.00 **PER BOOK** for shipping and handling.

The Cartel Publications * P.O. BOX 486 OWINGS MILLS MD 21117

Name: _____

Address: _____

City/State: _____

Contact/Email: _____

Please allow 5-7 BUSINESS days before shipping.

The Cartel Publications is NOT responsible for Prison Orders rejected, NO RETURNS and NO REFUNDS.

NO PERSONAL CHECKS ACCEPTED

STAMPS NO LONGER ACCEPTED

By **T. STYLES**   297

CPSIA information can be obtained
at www.ICGtesting.com
Printed in the USA
LVOW11s1829271017
554039LV00001B/74/P